TATTOOZ II

Is it true what they say: if you can't trust family who can you trust

WRITTEN BY LYNNE MACK

TATTOOZ II

Copyright © 2025 by Lynne Mack

First Edition

ISBN: 978-0-9886119-1-7 (Print)

Cover Design: Markee Books

Interior Design and Layout: Markee Books

Published by: Lynne Mack

This book is a work of nonfiction. Names, characters, events, and incidents are either the products of the author's imagination or used in a fictitious manner. Any resemblance to actual persons, living or dead, or actual events is purely coincidental.

CONTENTS

PROLOGUE

The two cars sped down the street side by side for two blocks. Fielding was in the Mustang, in the Mercedes Benz was an unknown driver. Both were high-powered, sleek, and too damn good-looking to get wrecked—but that's exactly what was about to happen.

In the Mustang, Fielding's phone rang.

"What?"

"Hey, where are you?"

"I'm in a bit of a jam. What's up?" It was Sam one of Fielding's workers from the business.

"Some guy's been asking around about you."

"Ok?"

"I just think you should be careful."

BLAM! The Benz sideswiped his Mustang.

"Really?"

BLAM! Fielding swerved back into the Benz, making a deep dent in the driver's side.

"What's all that noise? What are you doing?"

"Driving."

The dark-tinted window of the Benz began to roll down slowly. The barrel of a gun appeared.

"Boom."

"Eh, look, I'm kind of busy right now. Can I call you back?" Fielding asked.

"Sure, man. Call me back."

"Hey."

"What?"

"Stay safe out there."

"Yeah, right." Fielding ended the call.

They were on a one-way street. Déjà vu hit Fielding like a jolt. Had he been here before? He yanked the wheel and spun his car into a 360, smashing the Benz head-on. Boom! The Benz flipped once, twice, and landed upright. The car was banged up from top to bottom. The roof was caved in, the doors were smashed.

Fielding got out of his vehicle, unscathed and masked, a gun in hand. He walked with the authority of the gods toward the wrecked Benz. The barrel of a gun emerged again from the driver's side.

"This motherfucker," Fielding muttered. "I was going to go easy on you, bitch," he said, as his feet landed in front of the car.

He opened fire, unloading the entire magazine into the car. When the clip was empty, he approached and checked for signs of life. None. The man was dead.

He climbed back into his car, sirens wailing in the distance.

"Now the only question was," Fielding thought, "who sent this man to kill me—and why?"

He drove back to his condo on the other side of town. He parked underground, and took the elevator to the penthouse. He owned the entire floor. He stepped off the elevator and went into the bathroom. He still had his face covered by his full black mask. He took it off and began washing the blood off of his face, then he stripped down from the bloody, torn clothes from the accident and got into the shower. He let the water run down his body and felt relief for a brief moment.

CHAPTER ONE

GO WITH YOUR GUT!

Go with your Gut! It's never what you think. It's always what you *feel*, Fielding thought. Go with your gut every time—in a business like this, or any kind of business—you have to know who you can trust. And most of the time, you can only trust yourself.

Over the past two years, Fielding had grown into a tall, striking young man. More handsome than before, if that was even possible. His light brown eyes had seen the darkest moments of his life, memories that clung to him like ghosts. They shaped how he moved through the world.

Since arriving in Philadelphia, Fielding had killed more people than he could count. He didn't want to continue down that path. He knew exactly what he wanted now: Children. Lots of them, all with one woman. Not like his father, who had kids with various women. Fielding envisioned a long lineage—children, grandchildren, even great-grandchildren.

He imagined her now. She would come back to him. He'd be at The Olde Bar and Grille—his favorite spot, partly for the food, mostly for the drinks.

In each glass, of alcohol she lived. He couldn't wait for the liquor to roll down the back of his throat because then he would be with her again. A portal of some sort. Taking him back in time. He was there now.

She would walk in a room and her entrance stopped every man in the room—even those sitting with other women. Fielding stayed still until she sat directly across from him waiting to hear the sultry words from her again.

"Fielding, move the fuck over."

It was his brother, Jake.

Jake had a knack for ruining every great moment.

"You could try being polite, bastard."

"I think you got that backwards, Jake grunted, shooting him a grizzly look, "just move."

Fielding slid over on the church pew. Jake sat down.

The church was packed. Flowers filled the altar. People who had known Sean Damino filled every seat.

Sean's gone now, Fielding thought. *He can't see any of these flowers.*

Gracie, Jake's wife, came in and sat down next to her husband. She didn't take up much space at all; she had lost a lot of weight and now looked as skinny as a twig.

"Where's the kids?" Fielding asked. Jake and Gracie had two little girls Diamond and Justine.

"Oh, I didn't want to bring them I figured that they are so young, they would be all over the place." Gracie explained.

Today, she was playing the role of the dutiful wife, perfectly. There were so many people that Fielding had never met at the funeral – like an old woman who needed assistance to walk, and a much younger woman who held her up by wrapping her arm inside of the older woman's.

"Who are they, Jake?"

"Oh, that is Aunt Freda and her daughter, I don't remember her name." Jake replied. "I hear she is really sick now, Parkinson's."

Then there was a tall man that Fielding spotted over in the corner leaning up against the wall looking like he wished he could disappear inside of the sheetrock.

"Who is that?" Fielding asked.

Jake sighed "What is this Family Ancestry Trivia? I don't know who that is," Jake said after turning his head around slightly to see who Fielding was talking about. "You know Dad knew a lot of people." Fielding began to realize that Jake was as much in the dark as he was when it came to his family history. Like him, Jake didn't know half the people at his father's funeral.

So, when people came up and said hello to Jake and said that they hadn't seen him since he was little. Jake would just say hello and smile politely.

Fielding couldn't wait for the charade to be over. When family members saw Fielding, they smiled and shook his hand then walked away whispering to each other, "That must be the other son."

Sean was buried in a closed casket there was a picture of him that stood off to the side. Jake sat silently all he really wanted to do was to mourn his father in solitude. He had felt really bad that the last time he had seen his father they didn't say much to each other.

The preacher gave a great sermon and many people shed tears for Sean. After the funeral, there was the procession with over a hundred cars. There was a police escort that went ahead of everyone and then one after the last car. There were people from the music industry, the publishing world, and television reality shows. Guests flew in from all over the states including California, Florida, and Las Vegas, Nevada. All to attend the funeral of the great Sean Damino, musical mogul. That was the same way it was when Sean was alive, they would fly into a party or Sean was flying out to a party. Now they were here to bury him.

Fielding still couldn't understand how his father could have died in a car accident. He didn't get much information from the detective, and it all seemed suspicious to him, that they ruled out any foul play. Everyone knew Sean was one of the most notorious criminals on the East Coast. He had a lot of enemies.

They said he was driving pretty fast and with it being dark and rainy, it appeared that he had spun out on a winding road. He had flipped his tiny sports car a couple of times before it exploded in flames. The coroner's report said that witnesses had said that he had had been drinking heavily right before he got into the car.

Fielding felt especially bad because he had just gotten to know his father and now, he was gone. He never imagined things ending so soon. He had lost so much already, his real mother who he had just found out about had died several years before he arrived in Philadelphia and the woman who raised him who he believed to be his mother had died two years ago, and now… Sean.

"Maybe we should go to therapy." Fielding said at the cemetery standing next to Jake.

"Therapy, why? You crazy?"

"A little, aren't you?" Fielding locked eyes with his brother. "That's not what I'm talking about. "I mean grief therapy is supposed to help people get through a loss."

"I'm not grieving. Besides, my blunts will do just fine, if I'm feeling melancholy."

"That isn't the answer man when you come down off that high, where are you? Right back where you started from." Fielding said.

"Oh yes, I know this, that is why there is plenty of that where this one came from," Jake said laughing as he lit up his joint.

Fielding shook his head at his brother.

Gracie had tried several times to speak with Fielding at the funeral.

She figured while they were outside it would be the perfect place to talk to him. Gracie had been getting skinnier and skinnier. Fielding was sure she was hooked on the pipe. Although when he asked her about it, she denied it. But now it was in her eyes too. She couldn't hide it anymore. Jake wouldn't notice anything about his wife even if it hit him smack between the eyes. That's because Jake was always in his own world, which included getting high, sleeping with other women, and watching television. Jake was a bum especially since he hadn't made it to the NFL as he had planned. Since then, he hadn't been interested in doing anything except ruining his life.

Gracie managed to hike through the muddy lawn to get next to Fielding and strike up a conversation, but all Fielding could remember was his last talk with her when he really tried to break it off. The E&J was calming his spirit as he continued to remember as if he were still there.

While Jake moved forward to pay attention to what the pastor was saying. Fielding stepped back away from the crowd to talk to Gracie.

"What do you want from me, Fielding?" Gracie had asked.

"What do I want? You know what I want."

"You want me to leave Jake?" she asked with her eyes doing a crazy acrobatic dance.

"When did I ever ask you to leave my brother?" He got closer to her. "I never asked you to do that. Jake is too fragile I just want you to be there when I call. You weren't there, Gracie, you were never there."

"I thought we were over." She moved a hand between her and him back and forth. "I thought this was over."

"Sean is dead, Gracie. All bets are off, and you know I have always wanted you. But I love my brother and I love you too. I don't want to let either of you go."

***

He remembered they had another conversation at his condo not that long ago, very similar to the one she was trying to strike up here out in public, but it didn't end very well.

"What about Laurel?" Gracie had asked.

Fielding gave Gracie a dry look because she knew that he and Laurel were not together but he decided to remind her anyway, "Laurel, left me, Gracie. You know that." Fielding poured himself a drink.

"Yeah, but she still loves you."

"She may, but that is not the situation here. She has nothing to do with us." After a pause he said, "Come here."

"What you want Fielding? For me to suck you off? Get one of your whores to do that!" Gracie exclaimed, crossing her arms across her body as a stance of defiance.

Fielding laughed and then smirked. Gracie, you are one of my whores."

Gracie heard something sinister in his voice, and then she saw it in his eyes too. Who was this man that she had allowed to crawl back into her life? He was not the same boy she met just a short time ago, on the basketball court when they were just innocent young kids. No, this man was different.

He gave her a look that said, I rule you, and his stern direct voice even commanded her, directed her, "Come here."

Fielding sat down in a chair as Gracie moved closer to him. He spread his legs apart. She knelt down in front of him and began to fiddle with the zipper to his pants. She looked up at him with sad eyes; he looked back at her with empty ones. She began to put her hands down his pants. He put his hand on hers making a gesture for her to stop. She had always enjoyed making Fielding happy, but now something had changed, and Fielding was now a dictator and she didn't know how she was going to handle that. He had once been her savior and now he was her captor. She moved his hand so she could continue. He moved his hand on hers, more demanding this time, and shoved her hands away.

"Stop," he said, pushing away from her and then getting up from the chair.

Gracie rolled off of her knees and sat back on her butt wondering what he was doing. Did he finally remember that he had a conscience?

His phone started ringing. She figured she should leave while he was taking the call. Her emotions were conflicted, she felt embarrassed, and at the same time used. She got up and started towards the door, trying to get out before he realized that she was gone.

"Gracie," Fielding called to her. She turned briefly. "I'll call you," he said in that same sinister voice again. That voice scared her and she couldn't wait to get away from him.

She opened the door and walked out on the other side of the door and then leaned back up against it fell to the floor and began to cry. Who was this man? He was not the Fielding that she had once loved. He was turning into a monster, or maybe she was the one turning into the monster. She was becoming someone even she didn't want to know. He was once sweeter and more sensitive than his brother and nothing at all like his ruthless father, but now he was worse than both of them had ever been. She wiped the tears from her eyes got up off the floor and then walked down the hall with a heavy weight on her shoulder. As she walked, she could see her pitiful self through the full-length mirror along the walls. What was she becoming she wondered. Her figure had changed; now she even recognized that she was thinner than she had ever been, her face stained with tears, and her head all mixed up. She had to get out of there and find her way back to her husband.

Back behind the closed door, Fielding had stepped into the bathroom then went to his personal bar and poured himself a drink. The feeling was so awesome he didn't even care what Gracie was thinking. She was just another ho to him now. He had loved her at one time, but he wasn't going to let his feelings get in the way. He knew to stay in this game, love couldn't be a factor.

Gracie was still standing next to him saying something. What was she saying? He had no idea what Gracie was talking about, he had totally tuned her out, thinking about that past memory.

He did so mainly because he didn't want anyone thinking that they were having any kind of intimate conversation especially Jake who kept turning around looking for her.

Fielding turned to Gracie, coldly and said, "Your husband is looking for you," Then walked away from her, as if they were never talking.

She stood there by herself for a moment then became angry at his disrespect for her. She stormed off with her heels still getting stuck in the mud as she flounced back over to Jake.

They were lowering Sean's body into the ground. Gracie really didn't give a damn; in a way, she was glad to see Sean dead. He had caused her nothing but grief. He had run the family with an iron fist, demanding that everyone around him be a saint, and he was far from sainthood himself. He had fathered Fielding and Jake by two different women and God knows how many others. He pimped women out and did his dirt that he hoped no one would ever find out about. Many of those skeleton bones were being buried with him today but there were still many more waiting to fall out of the closet and Gracie knew it. Both of his sons had many secrets. Some of those secrets were to never be revealed because they could cause so much pandemonium in the family, and people could end up getting killed. As far as she was concerned, when it came to Sean Damino it was good riddance.

Fielding almost died when Sean pushed him out of a third-floor window. No one would know it today because his wounds healed. The Damino family were cold blooded and would kill kinfolk just as fast as they would a stranger. They believed in loyalty in a nonsensical kind of way and if you crossed that path then your name went on that incessant list of death.

He had watched as they lowered the body into the ground. He had decided to skip the repast he wasn't in the mood for more phoniness.

Fielding did still have some compassion although he rarely showed it now. He drove home on autopilot. He got out of the car mentally exhausted, opened the door to his condo, and began untying his tie with one hand. He threw his jacket on the sofa and headed straight for the kitchen. He opened up a cabinet and pulled out a bottle of vodka and laughed at his life and how ridiculous it was right now. Laughing was a hell of a lot better than crying. He pulled a small glass container out of the cabinet and poured the liquor in it.

Then he did something that he thought he would never do. He reached back up in the cabinet, remembering the last time his brother was there; he had left some cocaine ; He took out the small bag of white powder and he lined it up on the granite kitchen countertop. He snorted it. As the powder began to work on his system, his thoughts were all over the place and he couldn't focus.

How could he treat Gracie like that?

What was Jake going to do when he found out?

I really miss my wife.

Those thoughts roamed around inside of his head over and over until the drug took effect once he had sniffed all the lines and swallowed a few shots. He was feeling much better, in fact, right now nothing mattered.

He was sure he knew how to control the coke; he was sure not to let it control him. He had seen too often what happens to people who let it control them. He wasn't even worried about the alcohol; they were old buddies. It was the cigarettes. After finding a nice one in the corner of the pack, he dumped it into his hand, and lit it, and started to smoke.

When his phone, rang, he answered, "Yo"

"What up man?" It was Jake.

"Rough day today, burying Dad."

"Well, we got through it," Fielding said puffing on the cigarette and walking over to the sofa and falling into it.

"How about we get through it even better?"

"What you got in mind?"

"We got the bitches out on the street, man, our money is being' made without us, what do they call that, passive income, I'm looking' to get into something." Jake said.

"Like what?" Fielding was trying to let the drag from the weed increase his high.

"Don't matter, man, find some hoes, or some shit like that, you down?"

"Yeah, I'm always down."

"Swing by I'm already zooted."

"Give me twenty, I'm on it," Jake confirmed.

"I'll be here. Come on up when you get here."

When Jake got there, the music was blaring, videos played on the big screen.

Fielding attempted to get himself together when he saw Jake come into his home.

"Eh, and let's do this." He stumbled into the air, trying to get off the sofa. Jake was lit up too, so he didn't even try to help his brother.

"I got an idea," Jake said. "Let them come to us."

"You are so smart." Fielding looked at his brother through intoxicated eyes; as if what he just said was truly ingenious and not drug induced stupidity.

Nothing was quite clear to either of them right now, but what Jake had just said to Fielding sounded like the most incredible idea he had ever heard. He stood in amazement at how smart his brother was and said "Alright, you the man, you in charge." Fielding saluted him as if he were an officer in the military and then stumbled backward, falling back onto the sofa.

A video came on that seemed to have Fielding's full attention; women were dancing around in front of the camera half-naked. Fielding wasn't sure how much time had passed, could have been fifteen minutes or an hour, so he asked his brother, "Did you make the phone call?"

"I did," Jake responded coldly. Just then, there was a knock at the door. Jake smiled at Fielding.

Fielding got up to open the door.

Three beautiful ladies stood in front of him; one white, one Asian, and one black.

"Come on in," Fielding said and turned around to get a good look at their asses as they entered the apartment. Fielding utilized a professional interior decorator and it was adorned with beautiful leather chocolate furniture. On the walls there were pictures of actresses and singers; one of his favorites was that of Diana Ross. In this photo, she had a blowout afro. Fielding thought Diana Ross was one of the most beautiful singers of all time. He loved her in the movie Lady Sings the Blues, in which she played a drug-addicted Billie Holiday and Billy Dee Williams played her lover.

Fielding had gotten addicted to old films when he lived with Rita Carmen in Florida; that was her favorite past time listening to old-time music like Etta James and watching old-time movies with actors like Jimmy Stewart and Humphrey Bogart.

The party was on, and Jake began pouring drinks. The girls giggled and *oohed* and *ahhed* as they admired the condo.

Fielding had flat screen tv's playing videos all around the apartment. The Asian girl had just counted three of them for the fourth time and started giggling. "No-no, wait, let me do it again. One, two, three", she continued as she ran around the condo, locating one in the kitchen one in the living room, and one in the hallway, and when she found the last one in the bedroom, she came out with a breathless, "four".

Fielding had a Bose stereo system for his music and his kitchen was right out of an *Easy Living mag*azine with granite table tops and stainless-steel appliances and gorgeous floors in the kitchen and stunning hardwood floors throughout the condo.

The group and began to get closer as the music took over the air and began to permeate their senses while the alcohol took over their spirits. Jake took the party to another level when he brought the cocaine out and spread it on the table; they all took a hit. Fielding was sitting on the sofa with the white girl who looked like she might be a few years older than him. They danced to an old Stevie B song called Spring Love, and the Asian girl laughed the whole time. When the music slowed down, she began to get closer to Fielding, who found out her name was Sue Hong, and she was Japanese. She brushed up against his body with her pelvis, grinding on his and then finally kissing him.

Jake had the white chick and the black girl on the sofa. Jake in his inebriated state was now getting a kick out of watching them kiss each other.

Sue Hong had gotten so involved in kissing and grinding on Fielding that they ended up falling on the sofa with Jake and the black and the white girl. The girls giggled some more. Fielding and Jake gave each other a coy look so Jake announced that they were moving the party into the bedroom.

Jake pulled Fielding off to the side asking. "Hey where is that coke, I left here last week?

"You didn't leave no coke here, Fielding said, lying.

"Yes, I did man." Jake insisted.

"You are full of shit, man. " Fielding had snorted that coke earlier and he didn't want to get into a big thing about it so he figured he could bullshit his way out of this conversation and since Jake was pretty torn up it worked.

Fielding pushed Jake into the doorway of the bedroom. "Look at that man." The girls were all laying on the bed half naked fooling around with each other. "Get in there man, they are ready," Fielding demanded. Jake forgot all about the coke, looked at his brother then back at the girls smiled, and went barreling into the room jumping on the bed.

Fielding had a huge bed that fit them all. His high was coming down a little but he liked it that way; he never liked to be totally fucked up. He got on the bed with the rest of the party. Fielding was digging the black chick; Her name was Kelly; her ass was heart-shaped; and he couldn't get it out of his mind. Although he was used to girls with smaller asses; hers was not too big and not too small it was just right. He started kissing her first. Then he switched back to Sue Hong. The white girl, Ashley, got jealous so she decided to jump on Jake and began pulling down his jeans as she unbuttoned her blouse. Fielding was laying spread out on the bed as Kelly and Sue Hong began to unbutton his shirt and began asking about his tattoos.

Fielding had his wife Laurel's name on his left shoulder. He refused to answer any questions about that one, and they didn't press the issue. He had one that looked like chains that were now broken. He had a pair of wings and small barbells on his right shoulder, meaning he was strong and could handle anything. They talked about them, admired them, licked them, and kissed them. Ashley, was doing the same thing to Jake who was now down to his underwear. The three women were now totally naked.

Sex started with Fielding and Kelly first. Fielding had her on all fours and he was banging her from the back while Sue Hong was underneath her, and she was licking Kelly's breast. Ashley and Jake were on the other side of the bed having missionary sex. Then they switched partners. The brothers ended up having sex with each one of the girls. Condoms flew all over the place as they opened them up and carefully put them on each time. Sometimes the girls helped put them on and sometimes they did it themselves. For the next few hours, there was nothing but laughter, sex, drugs, and more sex.

The next morning, Fielding woke up first and looked around the room. What a mess, he thought. There were clothes everywhere, used condom wrappers, and cups all over the floor. He jumped up and started waking everyone else up and began hustling the girls out the door. As he walked from girl to girl one on the bed one on the floor, and another in a chair, he began to remember snippets of the night. He smacked Kelly on the ass.

"Get up. Come on, time to go" he said then went to the bathroom to brush his teeth. He looked around the corner of the door and came back out of the bathroom with a toothbrush in his mouth.

"Eh," This time, he smacked both Sue Hun and Ashley on the butt. "Get up. You got to go."

"Hey, what's the deal?" Sue Hun groaned.

"The deal is you got to go, now," he replied while biting down on his toothbrush trying not to let it fall out of his mouth. "Let's go." He said and then went back into the bathroom to spit in the sink. The girls were moving in slow motion but all the same, still moving. They began searching around the room looking for their shoes and hand bags.

"If we decide to party again my brother has your number, we'll call you," Fielding said coming back out the bathroom and moving them along and picking up articles of clothing that he knew did not belong to his brother and tossing it at them as he hustled them towards the front door.

"Hey" Ashley whined, "easy," catching a flying tank top in the face.

Fielding ignored her comments and continued pushing them towards the door. He managed to open it and reluctantly, all three walked out. . Still moaning and half-sleep, Fielding shut the door behind them.

Fielding returned to the bedroom where Jake was still sleeping, only, he wasn't on the bed; he was passed out on the floor. Fielding shook his head and stepped over his brother.

He decided to take a shower and figured by the time he was finished Jake would be awake.

"You want to hit the shower?" Fielding asked with a towel wrapped around his waist.

"Yeah, man," a groggy Jake said, massaging his head.

"You should call your wife." Fielding said.

"Oh, really." Jake laughed ignoring his brother's advice and brushing past him to get into the bathroom to shower.

"Don't take all day," Fielding yelled as Jake closed the door. Fielding got dressed in a pair of jeans and a blue T-shirt.

Fielding went into the living room and began checking emails on his computer. He looked at the time. It was after 1:00 pm.

"Jake, it's late. Come on, man, we got some errands to run."

Fielding continued to read some emails; he was hoping something would be there from Laurel, but there was nothing. By the time he was finished Jake was coming out of the bathroom. He had put the same clothes back on that he had on the day before.

Jake sat down on the sofa, pulled a joint from his pocket, and started smoking.

"Man are you ever not high?" Fielding asked.

"Yeah," Jake answered.

"When?" Fielding laughed, walked over to his brother, motioned for him to pass the joint and took a few puffs, and returned it.

"In my dreams."

"Exactly." Fielding replied, returning to the computer and sitting down.

"No seriously, in my dreams, I am a straight-up kind of guy, a true gentleman. Nothing like the ass hole I am in real life."

"Well good, nice to know that somewhere in the multiverse you're not a punk. Fielding took another hit and passed the joint back. They smoked in silence until it burned out. Jake lit another.

Fielding responded to emails until his phone began to ring. It was on the coffee table, just a few feet away but annoyingly out of reach.

Jake paused, recognizing the ringtone Rihanna's voice rang out "*You da one that I think of all-day*"

Fielding groaned. The music felt like needles.

Jake walked toward the singing phone. Fielding's high evaporated in an instant. He knew exactly who was calling. "*Your love is my love my love is yours*," Rihanna kept singing. Right now, Fielding hated Rihanna and wished she would just shut up. But she continued to sing the hook again. "*You da one that I think of all-day*." He looked at the phone and then looked back at Jake who was reaching to pick it up.

"No," he thought because he knew exactly who that ring had belonged to but so did Jake. Jake tapped the screen on the phone. "Hello," he answered, locking eyes with his brother.

Fielding inhaled deeply.

Jake knew whose number it was, even before he heard the soft female voice on the other end call his brother's name.

"Fielding?"

"No, baby, it's not Fielding," Jake said, his voice low. "Why are you calling my brother?"

There was no response. "That's okay, you don't have to answer. I already know. I'll see you when I get home."

In a rage, Jake hurled the phone across the room. Fielding ducked. The phone shattered against the wall pieces scattering across the floor.

"I'm not paying for that," Fielding joked, eyeing the dent in the drywall. "You know I'm not going to get my deposit back."

Jake was already charging. No longer the 260-pound quarterback, but still massive. Jake moved towards him quickly, put his hands behind his back. Fielding saw the .45 Jake pulled from the back of his pants.

Fielding moved fast, drawing his own revolver from behind his waistband. He always carried.

"Look, man, I can explain," Fielding said aiming his weapon.

"I should have killed your ass the last time! You still messing with my wife?" Jake roared.

"Let me explain." Fielding pleaded. Negotiation was his specialty.

Jake's face turned an alarming shade of red. Fielding thought his head was about to pop off.

"Look man, we're high. We drank too much. Let's put the guns down and talk. I don't want to shoot you and I don't want you to shoot me. But if you don't lower that gun in my house, I swear to God I'll put a bullet in your head."

Jake's grip loosened slightly. His breathing slowed. The rage started to drain from his face.

"Come on man, it's about to get really messy in here," Fielding said with a nervous laugh.

Jake finally lowered his weapon and shoved it back into his waistband.

"I see you got some heart now," Jake muttered, sinking onto the sofa.

"Damn, man," You pulled a gun on me in my house?" Fielding holstered his revolver but stayed alert. He sat across from Jake.

"Gracie's been coming over here, saying she still loves me and doesn't want to let go," Fielding began, "I told her it's over; we're done." He signed "finished" with his hands.

"I knew I couldn't trust that bitch." Jake muttered, fidgeting. "I'm going to kill her."

"No," "Fielding said, firmly. "Leave her alone. I told her it's over. Let me talk to her again- I'll tell her you know everything; I'll make sure she stops."

Fielding voice was calm but insistent. Despite everything, he still cared for Gracie. He couldn't let Jake hurt her.

Even though he was being mean to her now, He couldn't let his brother get violent. No matter what, she didn't deserve that.

Jake exhaled and looked at his brother that he loved, "You gonna to tell her it's done?"

"Si, mothafucker," Fielding replied. "I got you; I'll tell her tonight. She won't call again."

"All right." Jake said, stood and headed for the door. "I love you, man," he said, glancing back.

"I love you too," Fielding replied. "But Jake…"

Jake turned around.

"If you ever pull a gun on me in my house again you better make sure that you kill me."

"Right," Jake said with a smirk, then left. His only thought now was getting home to Gracie. He would keep his word-he wouldn't lay a hand on her. But he'd wait and see if Fielding held up his end.

In his bedroom, Fielding laid back on his bed, realizing just how dangerous this game had become. It wasn't just his life at risk anymore -it was Gracie's too.

He knew what he had to do; he was going to keep his promise to his brother. In one instance, he was this hard ass with everyone he met except with his brother and his father. With Jake and Sean, it was different. They were family. He loved them. And now that Sean was gone, his only family was Jake. So why did he keep hurting him? He tossed the question around in his head. Why couldn't he let Gracie go?

This life was unpredictable. Dangerous. And somehow, he liked it. The adrenaline. The risk. It was better than any sex, cocaine or alcohol. It was a rush. A game of sorts. Every day, he wondered: would this be the day he died?

Spread out on his bed he began thinking of Rita Carmen the woman he called Mother. The one who'd swapped him and Jake leaving them to grow up in a lie.

But still, he thought living with Rita Carmen wasn't always bad. There were some good times. It must have been so hard for her to love him, Fielding thought knowing the whole time that he belonged to another woman and the woman whom she had despised.

He had never known his biological mother, Chill. She was dead. He only knew Rita Carmen the unstable woman who dragged into this city. Three years after her death, he was still untangling the damage.

He knew that Sean Damino was a man who didn't play, he was very serious. He took his life and his business seriously. He wasn't rich when he was growing up. He grew up in very humble beginnings with a single mother, on welfare, and lived in the projects. His dream was to become a well-respected man in the community, and he achieved that all by himself. Sean Damino never knew his own father. His mother had told him that he was a married military man. When his mother found out, she was already six months pregnant. She made the best out of a bad situation as a single mother. She never heard from Sean's father again. He wanted to make sure that he didn't ruin his life with his wife so he made sure she never found out. But Sean's mother, Fielding's grandmother was not a stupid woman. She knew he was in the Army, and so she got in touch with the military and let them know about Sean and soon checks started coming. She was able to get off of welfare and bought her and Sean a little house. That stunt by Sean's mother sealed any possible relationship with Sean's father. After that he never wanted to see Sean's mother again. He was going to have to explain to his wife where that money was going.

He kept his promise; Sean never knew his father.

Fielding didn't know much about Sean's family. He knew even less about Rita Carmen. Even at the funeral, the family was distant. He wasn't sure who to ask, if anybody, about his father because everything was so secretive. Jake had grown up with Sean and didn't know much himself, they never visited family. Most people who came around Sean were his associates or lovers.

Fielding was starting to understand the traits Sean passed down. Strength, yes -but also addictions: to women, to power, to risk. It was in the blood.

Now, it was his biological mother that he wanted to know more about . He didn't know what his mother had passed down to him. What traits did he get from his mother? What part of him was her spirit? He wanted to know more about his mother Chill.

Sean got his strength from his mother. Sean passed that power down to Fielding. It was in the genes. But Fielding also got some bad habits passed down from Sean like his addiction to women and greed. That stuff was in him, it was in his blood.

He didn't care whose woman it was if he wanted her. If he wanted her, he'd take her.

There were certain types of women that Fielding couldn't resist. He liked the innocent look, the glasses, school teacher, or librarian vibe. Smart women were very sexy. But he also loved curves, swagger.

But more than all of that, Fielding wanted love.

And the love of his life was gone.

Could he ever get her back?

Would he ever love again?

CHAPTER TWO

BLACK COFFEE

"I never thought I would see you again," the woman said.

There was something about the way she said it, that made it all feel surreal.

"Yeah, well you know I have that effect on people," he said, with a smile.

He pulled her into his arms and held her as if he'd just been given back his life. As he embraced her, he felt his soul begin to breathe again. Her fresh clean scent filled his nose, immediately turning him on.

Fielding made love to her like a man headed for death row- passionate, desperate. He moved against her with a perfect mix of tenderness and urgency, drawing soft familiar sounds from her lips. Just as he was about to whisper how much he missed and loved her –

Fielding woke up in a cold sweat.

She wasn't there.

All he had was an erection and frustration. He slapped the mattress.

"Got damn," he muttered, then got out of bed.

He splashed cold water on his face, he grabbed his toothbrush, brushed his teeth, and then jumped into a cold shower. He tried desperately to shake his thoughts from the dream. Today, he needed clarity. No distractions.

He had to go to the office.

His fathers' will made him CEO of Tattooz Inc. Today, he planned to make good on that responsibility. Already late for a morning meeting, he jumped in his car and drove through the city traffic to the downtown office building.

He was going to have to get used to this new position of corporate CEO. Fielding was used to hustling on the street, now his hustle would be in the board room.

Sean had gotten into more sectors; he didn't just do music anymore. He had added advertising to his repertoire. Fielding was getting a crash course in business, but he was young, bright, and driven he wouldn't have any problem taking over the reins of the company.

Fielding wore a blue tailored suit that fit his body perfectly, he strode down the hall to the seventh-floor conference room, as he walked by each cubicle every woman stopped a moment to stare as the new young executive breezed by, some of the men even snuck a look. Fielding had presence.

The staff was already seated and waiting patiently in the board room. A presentation was scheduled for critique. He walked in apologized for his tardiness and sat down at the head of the large rectangular shaped conference table.

"I'm sorry I'm running late," he said surveying the room.

There were ten staff members there now all eyes glued on him. Jennifer, Angie, and Pamela from marketing. Paul and Denver worked upstairs in design. Three other women, Mrs. Pacer, Miss Wallace, and Brenda, all worked in finance. Tamir and Keyshawn were new to the organization, and they worked in the studio. The women smiled; the men exchanged glances. The tension was subtle but intense.

Sean had run a tight ship and Fielding planned on following in his father's footsteps. He wasn't letting go of his street side just yet either. He had employed street hustlers who were always on the grind. Silenced filled the room once he was seated at the front of the table. A skinny receptionist with braids approached Fielding's chair.

"Good morning, Mr. Michaels. How would you like your coffee?" she asked with a bright smile.

"Black is fine, Claire. " Fielding replied.

Jake slipped into the room without a care for timing. Fielding had hoped to get his brother involved in the business. – but Jake wasn't interested. He just wanted a check.

Jake sat beside Fielding.

"What up, man?" he said quietly.

"You're late," Fielding replied.

"Yeah, and what's going to happen, are you going to fire me?"

"Keep it up and that is right where you are headed."

Jake smelled like liquor. His eyes were bloodshot and sunken. Fielding sighed inwardly, disappointed again.

He buzzed the intercom. "Claire, can you bring another black coffee?"

"Sure thing," Claire confirmed.

"Thank you, "her rubbed his palms together. "Coffees are on the way, we're ready. Let's begin."

Brenda, the light-skinned woman from finance, stood up and made her way to the front of the room. Jake couldn't help but ogle her as she walked. Tight skirt, fitted blazer. Jake was obvious.

She began her PowerPoint presentation. Jake was bored almost instantly. Fielding masked his disinterest better but wasn't feeling it either.

Claire returned with two cups of hot coffee. Fielding thanked her, and she beamed. She was still excited to work there; most of her friends envied her.

"Thanks, Claire," Jake gave his brother a look, he was clearly amused by his inappropriate flirting. accepted the hot cup.

"Pay attention," Fielding chastised his brother.

Fielding thought Claire was cute too, but he wasn't mixing business with pleasure. He'd seen how that turned out for his father.

Years ago, Sean had an affair with a secretary who got pregnant. He urged her to get an abortion. She refused. Then she had a bizarre accident right outside the building. While walking down the street, a man on a bicycle had been speeding down the pavement and ran right into her, knocking her onto the ground. It was a bad fall, and the woman had a miscarriage. Sean paid her to keep her mouth shut about it. Although he could always deny that the pregnancy ever existed, he wanted to end their relationship on a good note, and he figured if he broke her off with some nice cash, he wouldn't have to worry about her.

And she wasn't the only one.

Sean had paid for multiple abortions. Jake told Fielding that their father had aborted at least twelve of his seeds. Jake had laughed, jokingly saying "less we have to share."

Fielding didn't know how to feel about his father's sloppy indiscretions.

By the time Fielding had finished his coffee Brenda was wrapping up her presentation. It hadn't impressed him. Fielding looked at Jake hoping to get his opinion, but with one glance, he could tell that he hadn't paid any attention at all.

"Thank you," Fielding said, please send your notes by email.

The staff began closing their laptops and whispering. Fielding heard bits of conversation.

"Her marketing strategies won't work."

"Where did she get those stats?"

"She used my picture without asking."

"Haters" Fielding thought.

Only he and Jake remained.

Jake leaned back in the chair.

"What?" Fielding asked.

Jake smirked "How does it feel?"

"How does what feel?" Fielding asked.

"Knowing that they all would sleep with you in a heartbeat."

"Everyone wants the boss. Doesn't mean it's a good thing."

"Really. Did you talk to Gracie?" Jake's tone shifted.

Fielding nodded "Yeah. Like I said- it's done." But he had not talked to Gracie. Fielding decided telling Jake exactly what he wanted to hear would be the best option for right now.

"Okay. I hope so Fielding." Jake said. "I don't want to have to talk to you about this again."

"You won't. Like I said, it's done." Fielding continued to allow his brother to think he was dominating the conversation.

Jake nodded.

"Come on, let's get out of here," Fielding suggested.

"Where are you on your way to?" Jake said.

"I need to check on some things at the condo, I'm a run by there, what about you?" Fielding said.

"No, I actually need to be somewhere else. I'll catch up with you later."

"All right," Fielding said.

"Okay, I'm out," Jake said and got up and left the board room.

Fielding thought about the lie that he had just told Jake. He was thinking he really needed to keep the promise that he made to his brother. First, he would see Gracie one last time, and then that would be it. He would end it.

At the Old Bar and Grille, Fielding met up with Alonzo who was tearing into some hot wings.

"Why you still fucking your brother's wife?" Alonzo asked between bites.

"Because I can," Fielding replied.

"Why you still living at your mom's house?"

"Because I can." Alonzo said, in between murdering those wings.

"Mind your business?" Fielding snapped.

Alonzo was muscle on his payroll. Jacked, short, with a mysterious Afro-Caribbean look. Swore he was Puerto Rican. Fielding didn't usually talk personally with employees, but Alonzo had become a friend, and in some ways a confidant.

"You love her?"

"Man, what you know about love?" Fielding said, laughing. He now saw Alonzo more like his conscious than an employee. "I dig her. It's more of an addiction. I can't stop. I can't let her go."

"You can't keep lying to Jake," Alonzo explained.

"You got a family?" Fielding asked.

"I got a girl, a couple of kids," Alonzo replied.

"You cheat?"

"Not anymore."

"Liar."

"Okay, but she is not my brother's wife."

"It's not that simple."

"Pussy is pussy."

"You don't even believe that," Fielding said. They both laughed.

"You think I'm selfish?" Fielding defended himself.

"I think you need to make a choice."

"I can't do that," Fielding admitted and took a cigarette out of his pocket and lit it up.

"Maybe you can't right now, but you will have too sooner or later." Alonzo got up from the table. Alonzo started to take some money out of his pocket. Fielding waved it off. "I got it."

Now that he was alone, Fielding stared at his large plate of food: roasted chicken, grilled vegetables and mashed potatoes, rolls and butter, and a large glass of sweetened tea. With a diminished appetite, he stared at his plate as if all the answers lay somewhere between the potatoes and the carrots.

Therapy. First, he had thought about grief therapy, but now he knew that kicking addictions was at the root of the problem, he should focus on that first.

He'd join every group there was so that he could kick all of his bad habits. He would join a smoker's group to stop smoking, he would join Alcoholics' Anonymous to stop drinking, and he would get a sex therapist to stop his sexual promiscuity, and then even admit that he did too much coke.

Fielding had been searching for an anti-smoker group on the internet for a while he had finally found one and signed up, the class would start tonight in person.

The room was set up like a classroom and the therapist stood in front while everyone else took a seat in front of her. The therapist Miss Mary reminded Fielding of a nerdy schoolteacher in her pink cashmere turtleneck and glasses. She probably went home and ate Chinese food while binge watching classic turner movies or reality TV shows.

During the class, Miss Mary lectured about the history of smoking and then finally talked about how it could lead to horrible conditions like emphysema, cancer, and even death. Fielding paid attention and was thinking about how he would begin to smoke one less cigarette every day.

The class had a mix crowd.

His first session was great. Fielding was looking forward to returning. The first day he stayed in the back and just observed. He thought to himself maybe next time he would get more involved and introduce himself to Miss Mary.

He had an alcoholics group on Wednesday nights, he wasn't quite sure if he belonged in this group. Fielding didn't consider himself an alcoholic but just in case he was on his way to becoming one, he thought that this would be a great intervention.

There was one guy who admitted to having gay sex only when he was drunk and he wanted to stop. Eventually, his wife was going to find out and it would ruin his marriage.

There was another man who said that he lost his whole family because of his drinking. One day, he came home drunk and lit up a cigarette and fell asleep in the chair. First, the trash can next to him caught on fire as he had the cigarette hanging between his fingers before it dropped down into the plastic can. The smoke woke him up, but before he knew it the chair, he was sitting in was on fire. He ran up the stairs to alert his kids and his wife and they all made it out in time but the house burned down. After that, his wife left him. Everyone's stories sounded so incredibly devastating and he began to believe that his life was just as screwed up.

He heard the story of a woman who said that when she was drinking, she didn't remember anything and walked the streets at night looking for money, which led to her selling her body. That eventually led to her doing drugs. The woman said she lost all her children to the foster care system and didn't know if she would ever get them back. Fielding spent time in foster homes and knew how lost he had felt as a kid and that kind of choked him up.

After class, Miss Mary asked Fielding to stay afterward so they could talk. She was about ten years older than him with long black hair, thin with no ass. She looked like a straight-up freak to Fielding. She said she noticed him get emotional as he listened to the stories and started asking him to tell her how those stories made him feel.

Fielding said it made him think about his childhood and how some of those stories were his stories, too.

Miss Mary nodded as he spoke. As she watched his lips move, it put her in a trance. In the middle of Fielding talking, she got up and planted a kiss right on his lips. She kissed him intently, lifting her leg up on his while they stood at her desk.

"Miss Mary." Fielding said. "Miss Mary."

"Oh," Miss Mary was startled She wasn't actually kissing this handsome young man, thank God. She had been fantasizing . Even though it wasn't really happening she was still embarrassed.

"I'm sorry, I just remembered I have to make a stop on my way home." Miss Mary had explained to Fielding as she began collecting her things.

"Oh, okay, I will see you next time." Fielding said as Miss Mary rushed out the door.

Fielding left out the building and found his car and sat in it for a minute thinking.

Why did he kill people?

In the beginning, it was business. But now it was kill or be killed.

He didn't want to do it anymore. There was too much blood on his hands. He'd try talking first. But he knew giving up one vice meant clinging harder to another.

He was taking over Sean's empire. Fast.

When he, let go of one thing, he had to replace it with something else. He was not that guy who could just go cold turkey. He had never been that guy. He had just gotten to learn the business before Sean died. He had to take a crash course in marketing and business. He spent a lot of late nights researching information on the internet and of course asking questions at work with the higher executives about the business. He was a quick learner and he was easing into the position that his father held for so long.

After his therapy class Fielding decided to drive to a late-night restaurant.

He called up Jake and told him where he was at and that he should come to have dinner with him.

"Que paso," Jake said to his brother. His Spanish was limited; he said a few words that Fielding had taught him.

"Nada," Fielding said. "Come and join me for some dinner. You know I hate to eat alone."

Jake arrived in thirty minutes.

Fielding had ordered a cranberry and vodka, and when the waitress brought it back to the table, Fielding took a gulp and said out loud to his brother, "So much for Alcoholics Anonymous."

"Why is that?" Jake asked.

"As you can see, I can't stop drinking?"

"Give it some time."

Jake sat down in the chair and let out a deep breath. "You know when it comes to eating there is no problem." Jake had gained a few pounds; Fielding had noticed that at the funeral. Now, he really saw that Jake was simply fat.

The waitress returned , to take Jake's order. "I'll have the wings and an order of tacos, the big burger, and fries," Jake ordered sloppily.

"Wings, tacos, burger, and fries?" Fielding questioned.

"Yeah, what's wrong with that?"

"Nada," Fielding returned.

"Hey, look, man, I eat what I want. You want to pretend you some kind of health nut go right ahead," Jake said as the waitress walked away. "But I don't see how you can be that healthy with the drug diet you on."

"That's my business."

"See… see." Jake started laughing. "Doesn't feel good, does it when the shoe is on the other foot? Don't judge me." Jake smiled a wide smile that showed his dimples. It was the one quality that Jake had left that made him quite appealing to the ladies. It was his gut that he needed to work on.

"You are still hitting the coke hard, aren't you?" Jake questioned, trying to sound concerned.

"I'm working on it. I didn't call you down to talk about my addictions. Don't you even know your own addictions.?"

"Yes, I do," he said to his brother as his food arrived then turned his attention to the waitress "Thank you," he flirted with the waitress and said, "I'm leaving you a big tip just for being this fine."

She giggled.

Fielding had a Caesar salad.

"You need anything else, gentlemen?" she asked.

"No, we're fine." Fielding jumped in, dismissing the waitress. He was ready to get down to business with his brother. "You haven't been over to the office since that last conference meeting two weeks ago."

Jake began eating his chicken. "Mmm, these are good," he said, half ignoring his brother. "I know I've been busy. Me and Gracie been going through something."

"You and Gracie always going through something," Fielding said. His food was still in front of him untouched.

"Are you going to eat man?" Jake said, chomping down on another chicken wing.

"Don't worry about my plate," Fielding commanded. "I need you at the office. I can't continue to hold things down on my own."

"So, what you want me to do?" He threw a half-eaten chicken wing back down onto his plate in disgust. "I told you when Dad died, I didn't want the business. You wanted to take on that load, you got it, work it out."

"Then I'm hiring a new manager," Fielding said.

"Okay, fine" Jake said and picked the wing back up and began putting hot sauce on it.

"I am running things on the street from up there on the 22nd floor." Fielding said.

"I watch the streets. You just collect checks, Fielding."

"That is what I'm supposed to do collect the money."

"I told you before, "I am not interested in the company. I'm not interested in that office or those hoes you moving around. You just keep doing what you need to do. I will do what I need to do."

"Oh, so I work for you now?" Fielding said.

"Whatever," Jake said.

"Whatever!" Fielding repeated. "See, that is what is wrong with you. You ain't shit but a washed-up quarterback who never made it to the pros, who found his solace in cocaine."

"Oh, and you don't?"

"I get high, when it's time to get high, I don't let my recreational activities interfere with my work. We got a business to run and you need to step up to the plate."

"Okay, fine. I'll step up."

"Good, be at the office tomorrow morning at 8:00 am sharp I need to go over some new deals that are coming through."

"Legitimate deals?"

"Are there any other kind?" Fielding asked, stealing a line from Jack Nicholson from *A Few Good Men*. "I need you to sit in on the meeting. We got some music producers coming to the table who are ready to put this new guy out. It's an investment for us, I want you to come to check him out. Besides, it would be nice for both of us to be there. It is a good look for business."

"Okay, I'll be there," Jake said now eating some of his nachos. He looked at his watch. "I got to go. You want the rest of these." Jake said, pointing at his plate.

"No," Fielding said turning up his nose and wondering why Jake even asked.

The waitress returned. "How was everything?"

"Great," Jake said, eyeing her cleavage. Her make-up was heavy as if she were about to go on stage for an off Broadway show and her hair was fake, cheap, synthetic that looked exactly what it was worth. Jake thought she was fine. "He pulled a one-hundred-dollar bill out of his pocket.

"Here you go, baby," Jake said. As she bent over, he pushed it down into her overexposed cleavage. Fielding watched his brother at work.

She pulled the receipt out of her apron and wrote something on it quickly and placed the bill upside down on the table. She smiled and walked sassily down the aisle.

Jake grabbed the receipt. Then showed it to his brother with a smirk on his face. "Told you man, this is me all day long."

"Yeah. Impressive." Fielding replied flatly.

Fielding liked his women a little less obvious and not so forward. He liked the hunt. Jake was lazy he liked women who were not a challenge. Jake had a beautiful woman sharing his bed with him every night. Fielding thought. Jake had no idea what he was giving up.

Jake left the restaurant happy and Fielding stayed quietly eating his grilled chicken Caesar salad. He called the waitress back,

"Can you bring me a coffee, black with sugar, please."

She said sure, walked away and left Fielding sitting at the table thinking about his next move.

CHAPTER THREE

PLAYERS STREET

The block had a dark mood. The spirits that haunted this street; were bold, daring and menacing. This was where people came to indulge themselves. No judgment, no snitches, no shame. Everyone knew what went on here. It was a place for secret sexual encounters and Fielding came because he was addicted.

People who recognized him didn't say a word. Most of the women there hoped that he'd choose them, but he only came for one woman and he knew she would be there.

The street's nickname, "Player Street," came from Arnoldo Famosa, the man who started it all. An immigrant from Cuba, Famosa began renting out a room in his home for extra money. Business boomed, and he bought another house, then another, the neighbors were so tired of the noise and the traffic they moved out one by one and eventually he owned the entire block. He considered opening a motel but decided that was too cliché'. This block, with its secrets and shadows, suited him better.

The strangest thing that most people wondered about was how did a Cuban immigrant find his way up north? Arnoldo never told that story. But he did say he could not go back down to Florida and that if he did, it would be the end of his life.

The city wouldn't officially rename the street, so the sign still read Charhill Street, but everyone on the street, knew it was Player's Street.

No one would know about it except people who had a need to know and they wouldn't talk unless they had an interested party who really wanted to come. It would become one of the biggest secrets kept throughout the city. This was a place where cheaters came to cheat and have fun.

Famosa, was now seventy-nine years old, was infamous- known as the Hugh Hefner of the ghetto. A lot of people called him Hughie and not Arnoldo.

He held secrets on nearly everyone from the mayor (who was afraid of losing the next election) to average family men (who was afraid of losing his wife and kids).

As long as he ran his houses discreetly and didn't interfere with the drug trade. He had the city in his hand and all he wanted was to run his houses and for the cops to leave his street alone and they did. In fact, no one messed with Hughie's business.

His clientele was discreet. Many were also looking to score drugs. One business fed into the other. Cops came too – off duty, married, but ready to cheat. Fielding had seen them often and the irony always made him laugh.

Fielding stopped in the office to talk to Famosa, who he now had in his pocket. Sean had him on his payroll for years, but now since everything had changed Fielding was running things. He made a lot of money from Player's Street.

"No one knew that Fielding was the money of this place, and he wanted to keep it that way, if people thought he was just a customer, that was the way he liked it.

The dirty cops tried to act like they are strait-laced people. Their wife is at home taking care of the kids and they are out playing while she is wondering if he's okay. Some of the wives are praying to God that their husband didn't get shot today, when in reality they were at Famosa's Player's Street knocking boots with some other chick.

Tonight, Fielding felt invincible, maybe it was the Hennessey, he had before he left the house whatever it was made him feel good. He saw people all up against the walls, laughing, touching, teasing. One guy caught his eye; he wore some jeans and a blue shirt with a collar. His face was round with a few freckles, low hair-cut. He knew that he recognized the guy but couldn't place his face. As he walked by the couple the girl gave him the eye while making out with him. After he was well past them, he remembered where he knew the guy from. He was a cop who worked the area at *Tattooz Inc.*

There was a couple on the sofa making' out, not paying attention to anyone. There were people standing and sitting on the steps that go upstairs to a few small bedrooms. The music in the house put him in a vibe. Couples were tangled on sofas. Women stared as Fielding walked through. He ignored them. He only wanted her.

Finally, he entered the kitchen. The kitchen air was smoky but not from cooking, but thick from weed smoke. He was getting a contact high as he walked through.

He spotted her standing near the back door to the screened -porch.

She was looking sweet to Fielding, like an innocent girl. He liked that. But still the way her body swayed in the doorway, he just wanted to grab her up in his arms.

She didn't say anything. Just looked at him as she usually did with those soft eyes that said I'm yours forever. He walked towards her and looked at her body then lifted her by the hips she wrapped her long legs around him.

She didn't know how close Jake had come to killing him over their affair. That was part of the thrill. The danger, it was more intoxicating than any drug. To know that his brother, her husband almost blew his brains out over their affair. That was the rush he got in doing these secret meetings.

He grabbed her neck with one hand and pushed her head gently up against the wall, kissing her. She was high, he could tell by her eyes. She wasn't looking at him; she was looking through him.

He pulled her close, put on a condom, overwhelmed by desire, and took her right there When she moaned, he covered her mouth. He thrust against her like a starving man. When it was over, she slid down the wall, breathless.

"Are you all, right?" he asked.

She nodded.

He took her arm and turned it over and saw neat tiny holes, one placed in front of the other, then he checked the other arm- they were identical.

"How long you been shootin' up?" he asked anger rising.

"You know." She said, and laughed.

He scooped her into his arms and carried her upstairs. He stepped over people who were making out on the steps.

"Excuse me," he said.

When he got upstairs, he placed her on a bed in an empty room. This time, he took his time making love to her, gentle, attentive, savoring, every touch and sound. She whispered that she loved him, that she was sorry. The rest were moans and breathless ecstasy.

They spent a few more hours there until their high dissipated then they left the house. It was still dark out although it was early morning. He carefully stepped over half-naked bodies everywhere in the house.

Gracie wanted to talk to him about their meetings and how she missed him but the drugs in her system wouldn't let her, it was as if her mouth had been wired shut. No words could come out, not the right ones anyway. Fielding tried to tell her that it was over and that he would never meet her at Player's Street again, but he couldn't get the words out either it was as if there was a spirit that held both their tongues and the words were lost.

"Will you call me, Fielding?" She asked.

"You know I will."

She walked away without looking back. He stayed and lit a cigarette, watching the sun rise. They never left together and always just as the night was turning to day. He would go his own way soon, but for now, he was going to smoke a cigarette. They weren't a couple. He blew smoke into the air and felt triumphant. He'd gotten through another night – alive-and it felt good.

***

Just as Fielding was about to walk back to his car. He saw the cop from yesterday coming out of the house, Officer Davis. He didn't notice Fielding, too busy trying to tuck his shirt into his pants and get out of there.

When Officer Davis did get home, he opened up the front door and found all the lights were off. He had gotten used to walking around in the dark and bumping into the kitchen chair and the living room sofa. He crept upstairs into his bedroom, slid out of his uniform down to his underwear, and slipped in between the sheets, and before he knew it, he was asleep.

Miss Mary opened her eyes as fast as he closed his and she just let the tears run down the side of her face. Her marriage was over she could feel it and she didn't know what to do with all her pain.

CHAPTER FOUR

23 DAYS

"It takes 23 days to kick a bad habit," Miss Mary was in front of the room explaining to the group. Fielding was looking at her and thinking to himself 23 days was a long time to go without smoking.

"But you see, while you are kicking the bad habit, you should replace it with something else ," Miss Mary said. "Let's just hope that it's something good, like a new found interest, art collecting, photography, something that is creative.

Fielding raised his hand. "Okay, I need to quit smoking."

"Why?" Miss Mary asked.

"Because they say that it is bad for you." Fielding teased.

"Who says that?" She asked.

"The Surgeon General."

Some people in the group chuckled.

"But what do you think?" Miss Mary asked.

"I think smoking anything is the best thing since sliced bread, especially after sex." Fielding smiled.

People in the group chuckled again.

The woman swallowed hard.

"Well, the thing is Mr....?" she questioned him.

"Fielding" he replied with a smile.

"Mr. Fielding," she continued

"Not Mister," Fielding interrupted. "Just Fielding."

"You have got to want to stop the thing. Everyone is here for different reasons, some want to quit smoking like you, others want to stop drinking, others want to stop gambling. But the key to stopping any bad habit is to really want to do it. So, my question to you Mr. Fielding is simple: Do you want to stop smoking?"

"Oh, yes, indeed, Miss Mary," Fielding said and rolled his bottom lip into his mouth with his tongue seductively and laughed to himself as he watched Miss Mary get flustered. Some of the students noticed and chuckled some more.

She turned away quickly, straightened her back, and faced the group again. "Good session, everyone, that's all for the day. "she said. "I will see you all next week."

The class got up quietly and began to exit the classroom, wondering why she had ending the class so abruptly.

Fielding remained in his seat.

One of the female participants from the group walked over to Fielding. She was Caucasian and tall with shoulder-length hair, looked to be in her twenties.

"Some of us are getting together tonight to have a no-smoking party," she said, smiling, "and I wanted to extend the invitation.

"Thanks," Fielding said, "but I think I'll pass." He looked over at Miss Mary.

The woman looked over at Miss Mary, too, and scoffed.

Miss Mary had stopped what she was doing and looked toward Fielding and the young lady. When Fielding looked at her, she quickly looked back down, fell down in her chair and began fumbling with papers on her desk.

Fielding got up from the chair and walked over to Miss Mary, who was now searching intensely for something in a lower desk drawer.

"You need some help, Miss Mary?" Fielding teased. He knew that Miss Mary was attracted to him; he figured it had probably been a while since she had sex the way she was now fidgeting in her chair.

"No, I don't," she paused, then added, "do you need any help" Miss Mary looked up quickly at Fielding, meeting his eyes then she looked back down at the floor.

"No, did you lose something?"

"My bag," she said looking down at the floor. "I'm looking for my pocketbook." She sounded frustrated.

Fielding looked at the chair that Miss Mary was sitting in and noticed a small handbag. "Is that it hanging on the back of the chair behind you?"

Miss Mary turned around quickly and saw it, took in a deep breath, and said, "Thank you."

Fielding stepped closer and reached behind her and unhitched the bag from the chair. "Here it is." He showed her the bag, and she grabbed it from him. Fielding chuckled. "Come on, let me walk you to your car."

In a stuttered whisper, Miss Mary said "Okay," and Fielding escorted her out of the old building.

He held the door for her, like a perfect gentleman.

Miss Mary looked at him with a raised eyebrow as if impressed. "Are you really trying to stop smoking, Mr. Fielding?"

"Please… call me Fielding," he said. "And the answer to your question is yes. I am really trying to stop smoking."

Miss Mary looked into Fielding's eyes and smiled. They were the most beautiful eyes she had ever seen. She tried to keep her composure and not let this young man see that he was making her feel something that she hadn't felt in a long time, flustered and aroused. It was clear to Fielding by the way she kept avoiding his gaze.

Fielding looked around "Where is your car?"

Miss Mary popped her forehead with her palm. "Oh, I forgot," she said, looking embarrassed. "I didn't drive today." She had totally forgotten that she had taken the bus that morning. Her car was making some funny noises so she left it with a mechanic shop so they could take a thorough look at it and fix whatever the problem was meanwhile she was going to take the bus to work. This morning she was running late she got halfway down the street when she realized that she had left her tuna fish sandwich and spring water bottle on the kitchen table and turned around to get it, by the time she got back in the house picked it up her bus was on its way down the street and she found herself running to catch it. How could she forget that?

"My truck is right there, Fielding said. "Let me take you home. I don't think you should be waiting on a corner for a bus this late."

She looked at him, and thought better of it; she barely knew Fielding. After looking at him for a moment, she took a breath and said, "Okay."

They walked a few more paces over to his truck. Fielding opened the door for her, helped her up into the vehicle and then jumped in on the other side.

Once he got behind the wheel, he asked, "Which way?"

"I'm up in the Northeast."

"Not a problem," Fielding said and then turned on a CD. He played some soft R & B music for her to relax. It took about twenty-five minutes to get to her home. Fielding pulled up right in front of her door.

"Do you mind if I use your bathroom?" Fielding asked when they got there. He hadn't realized until they parked that he really needed to piss.

"No, it's fine," Miss Mary said.

He jumped out of the driver's seat and went to open Miss Mary's door and help her out of the truck . She slid down the seat, it was a high step. The way she slid down she felt Fielding's body; a sigh slipped from her.

It had been a long time Miss Mary had been intimate with a man. She no longer had a sexual relationship with her husband even though they lived under the same roof. She had begun to throw herself into her work. She had been seriously thinking about divorce.

Fielding watched as Miss Mary unlocked her front door. She fumbled for a minute and then finally it opened she walked in and placed her bag on a chair. Her home was nicely decorated, and the living room was immaculate with everything was in its place. The furniture didn't look brand new but was very well kept. The kitchen had a breakfast counter with black bar stools up against it. A gray and white cat jumped off the sofa as Miss Mary ran around turning all the lights on. The cat ran behind the bookcase.

"Any more of those around?" Fielding asked, referring to the cat.

"No, just the one. Why? You don't like cats?" Miss Mary said.

"Not really." Fielding smiled.

"Her name is Lucy, and she is not very sociable, she won't come out when other people are around." Miss Mary confessed. "She only loves me."

"I understand," Fielding responded and smiled at Miss Mary.

"Um, the bathroom is right down the hall." Miss Mary pointed down a short narrow hallway.

"Okay," Fielding said, looking to the left in the direction that Miss Mary had pointed.

As he walked towards the bathroom, he yelled back at her. "You live here alone?"

"Yeah, it's just me." Miss Mary lied. "Her husband had just left town for some training for a few weeks.

Fielding stepped into a very clean, but small bathroom. He used the toilet, washed his hands but didn't see a towel to dry his hands so he opened the cabinet underneath the sink thinking there may be one there, and when he did, he got an eye full. There was a small vibrator in a box. Fielding chuckled to himself. He didn't find anything to wipe his hands on so he dried them on his jeans and emerged out of the bathroom back into the living room.

"Well, thank you," he said, "I don't think I would have been able to make it home without draining the dragon."

Miss Mary was sitting on the sofa, looking a bit more relaxed. She stood up to walk him over to the door.

Fielding was about to walk out when he turned around to Miss Mary who was right behind him. She hadn't expected him to turn around so quickly she thought she had time to move out the way. Before she could step back Fielding said to her, "Don't you get tired of doing that by yourself?"

"What are you talking about?"

Fielding explained, "In the bathroom, under the sink, that thing can't possibly satisfy you."

"It works." Miss Mary said now fully understanding what Fielding was talking about. She lowered her gaze and felt embarrassed. She hadn't taken out her friend since her husband went out of town. It was the only time she could get any pleasure because he wasn't giving it to her.

"Yeah." He kissed her on the cheek like a schoolboy "You sure about that." he whispered in her ear.

Once Miss Mary felt this young man's body closer to hers and could smell his fresh-smelling cologne and the touch of his lips still lingered on her cheek. She wanted him to do it again. She didn't move away as her mind told her to. She stood there waiting for it to happen again.

Miss Mary was at least twelve years Fielding's senior. She had never cheated on her husband not that the thought had never crossed her mind. But now she was feeling something that was driving her insane. She had always been a proper lady and a dutiful wife.

She had seen plenty of young men come and go in her classroom. And often she would get a little tingly feeling in her groin. If she would make it in the house before her husband, which was most of the time she would use her mechanical friend to settle that sensation. Each time she would use it she was thinking about one of those young men. She felt ashamed, exposed. But now with this young man, as sexy as he was in her home it was a fantasy come true for her. She could do nothing, her body was melted into the fabric of the walls. And she did believe that he could in fact read her mind.

The door never opened for Fielding to leave. Instead, Miss Mary found herself doing something she had only daydreamed about, she was kissing this young man and backing up down the hallway into her bedroom. Miss Mary had a large queen size bed that they toppled onto. Fielding pulled off his shirt and then began unbuttoning hers. As he did her breast emerged as two beautiful full-sized melons just right for the sucking. Miss Mary didn't say no to anything, she allowed it all to happen. He pulled her panties down underneath her skirt her body shivered with excitement and she helped him undo his belt buckle. Their clothes not even completely off, Fielding pulled a condom out of his pocket put it on quickly and mounted her, and began to pleasure her deeply. Miss Mary moaned liked an alley cat in heat. Fielding thought to himself *I knew she was a freak.*

After the first round, they both stripped completely and did it again. By the time the morning came, Miss Mary was up early fixing breakfast. She wore a very beautiful short pink robe that came just beneath her hips with nothing underneath. Fielding rolled over and looked at his watch it was 9:30 am on a Saturday morning he jumped up, pulled his jeans on with no drawers, and met her in the kitchen.

"Um," he said smells good in here." He was ready to eat. He walked over to Miss Mary and gave her a kiss "good morning."

She looked even more beautiful in the morning, her hair uncombed, but laid nicely around her face. Her glasses were nowhere to be found. Mary put breakfast on the table. Eggs, bacon, toast, and home fries. Fielding walked behind her and began pressing his pelvis on her ass and kissing her neck. She continued to pretend he knew he was probably shocked by the move and didn't know how to respond.

Fielding looked over Mary's shoulder at the bacon on the plate and said, "I don't eat the pig, baby."

"Oh, I'm sorry" Mary apologized as she grabbed the plate and began quickly scraping the bacon off back into the pan.

Fielding grabbed her hand. "Slow down, baby. It's okay. I think we know each other a little better than that now. You ain't got to be nervous."

"I know," she said. "I just am. I never…"

Fielding cut her off. "You never what?" he said to her then they both started laughing. Fielding began kissing her again. Her lips were very sweet. Then Mary did something that Mary never thought she'd do in a million years. She had not even done this with her husband in all the years she had been married to him. Mary dropped down to her knees. She began unzipping Fielding's pants and when she found his penis which was now long and hard in an instant it made Miss Mary get even more excited.

She started to suck long and hard on his pretty penis. Fielding rubbed the top of her head caressing her as she pleasured him. Miss Mary sucked his manhood with passion. She wondered, who is this woman? What am I doing? But with all her intelligence and self-talk she did not stop. When Miss Mary was through, she got up and began to warm up his breakfast. Fielding zippered up his pants and stumbled back over to the breakfast table.

"So, you gonna help me stop smoking?" Fielding asked Mary as they both sat on the sofa Fielding's chest was bare and he was smoking a cigarette.

"Absolutely," Mary said with all good intention. "Are you coming to class tomorrow night?"

"Oh yeah, I will be there. I got to stop smoking these things." Fielding said, putting his cigarette in an ashtray. "It is such a bad habit." He added. As he put the cigarette out, he noticed a picture on the table next to him it was a picture of someone who looked familiar to him.

"You know I don't even know your name."

"Mary," Miss Mary said. "My name is Mary." She smiled at him.

"No, I know that. Your last name. What is your full name?"

"Oh, she chuckled Davis, Mary Davis."

"Fielding's body went cold."

Looking sheepish, she added "I should have told you last night or maybe even this morning." She tilted her head toward the frame. "That is my husband,"

"Husband?" Fielding said, trying not to seem alarmed. It was bad enough that he was already sleeping with one married woman his brother's wife. But two? Besides, when was Mary planning on telling him, when her husband had a gun pointed to his head?

"Where is he?"

"Don't worry." He's not here. He is out of town. I found out that he was cheating on me. It's not the first time for him and I'm sure it won't be the last. I'm tired of dealing with it, and I don't think he even loves me anymore. I think I'm just a habit to him now."

"Well, people shouldn't be considered habits." Did he just say that Fielding thought. Who was he to be giving any kind of advice on how to treat people especially women.

If Mary only knew.

Fielding took another look at the picture, thinking again that he knew that face from somewhere.

Mary changed the subject. "What other bad habits do you have?"

"None, that I can think of." Fielding lied but knew the one bad habit that he really needed to kick was sleeping with all these women. Married women.

"You sure?"

"Yeah, I'm sure." Fielding gave her a look that said stop probing. "Besides, if I did, I don't need you for that."

"Okay," Mary said putting her hands up in the air in surrender. The one thing she did not want to do was piss off her new lover because she definitely wanted him to come back.

Fielding looked at her and smiled. "Twenty-three days?"

Her eyes lit in understanding.

"Twenty-three days," she confirmed.

"Okay, then I should be able to do that in less than a month."

"I think you can do it." Mary smiled back, now not sure if she would ever see him again.

"I think so, too." He said then got up from the sofa and kissed her on the lips. "I got to go." He announced.

Mary looked sad. "Will you call me later?"

"Yeah, I will." Fielding lied; he had no intention of calling Mary later. The next time he would probably see Mrs. Mary Davis was never.

CHAPTER FIVE

FAMILY REUNION

There were flowers everywhere. That was an odd thing for him to do he was not a flowery type of guy. He never sent women flowers. He would give jewelry, diamond rings, bracelets, earrings things like that, but never flowers. Because they didn't last. They died.

Today, he was looking at all kinds of flowers, trying to pick out the most beautiful but they were all so pretty how could he choose, he walked past them and smelled them each one more beautiful than the last.

Finally, he saw the most beautiful flowers he had ever seen. There were a mix of orange, yellow and green and all kinds of flowers dandelions and sunflowers. Wild and radiant. He reached out wanting to grab the arrangement before anyone else did.

Then, he felt extremely cold and opened his eyes.

He was in his own bed.

Alone.

He had been dreaming.

Fielding's day started off bad and just got worse.

When Darryl brought him the till for the day before, it was at least one-third less than usual. It didn't make sense, and Fielding could smell a rat.

Everywhere Fielding went that day, he felt like someone was following him. Like a spirit or a bad omen. Finally, he got in his car to go home, the phone rang.

"Fielding?"

"Yeah. who's this?"

"It's Mark, I'm new on the crew. They told me to call you."

"They who?"

"The guys- Alonzo and Darryl?"

"Okay, so what's up?"

"You need to get to 23rd and Diamond. Right now."

"Why, what's up?" Fielding said. He was smoking a cigarette and blowing the smoke into the air.

"It's Gracie, man, I think she's dead."

"What, what are you talking about?" Fielding sat up, quickly, stubbing out his cigarette. Where did you say you were?

"Twenty-third and Diamond."

"I'm on my way"

His mind went blank. Maybe it was a mistake. A prank. He didn't even know that guy, what did he say his name was, Mark?

The last time he saw Gracie, was on Player's Street, she was on her way home. They had such a good night, even though she was high, in the morning she had sobered up and called him the next day.

"Okay, so we are going to tell him." she was saying.

"Tell him what?" Fielding said, getting angry. "Tell him what, Gracie?"

"That it's gonna be you and me, together."

"I never said that I don't love you, Gracie, I do love you but we can't do this anymore. Why are we having this conversation?"

"Yes, we can, we can be together, we were always supposed to be together, remember. I need you, like another hit. Man, you are it for me." She pleaded sounding like a true junkie.

"I can't continue to hurt my brother like that."

"What you doing now? You are killing him now. When he finds out we both been lying to him for this long, he is going to flip, and you know it," she said.

And it made so much sense. But still, he knew it couldn't happen.

"No. Gracie. This is it. This is all we got, quickies at Player's Street, coke, ganja, and lies. That is, it, baby girl. I can't do it anymore."

"No." she screamed into the phone.

"Gracie," Fielding said, "the last time was the last time. It's over." She knew he was serious. "What?" Was this the end of it for real, was this the end of her lifeline. No, not this way not today she thought. Any day other than this day, another day, someday far away from here just give me one more day .

Gracie had hung the phone up on him. About twenty minutes later he heard a knock at his condo door, it was Gracie. He let her in.

Bad move. But he couldn't have the conversation outside.

She made her stance again against her lover this time in person. She felt as if she was holding on to a cliff and he was letting her fall by lifting one finger loose at a time.

"Oh, yeah you gonna get out of here," he said." He put the cigarette he was smoking in the corner of his mouth and held it tightly between his lips. He picked her up and threw her over his shoulder. She had remembered plenty of times when he had picked her up and laid her down to make love to her. This was not the same she couldn't understand it now. Her thoughts were all over the place, and she couldn't control them. He took her over to the front door of his condo.

"No, put me down," she yelled kicking him in the chest and pounding on his back. Right now, he didn't feel anything. He didn't want to do this, but he knew if he didn't, someone was going to get hurt. He didn't want anything to happen to Gracie. He wasn't worried about himself. And underneath it all, he truly loved his brother. That was all he had now.

He opened the door. He picked her up, to toss her out, but she wiggled out of his grip to the ground. She scrambled back up now in front of the door still inside of the condo. He tried to open it but she was batting his hands away each time he tried to pull the door open.

"Stop it, Gracie, get out." It was the way they had sex, aggressive, but this was not sex; this was the end of an affair. This was two lovers saying goodbye in the worst way possible. Gracie was crying and screaming. Fielding heard some footsteps coming towards his door.

"Fuck," he said. Someone had called the police. Gracie was still up against the door when they knocked on it.

"Police!"

Fielding looked back over at the coffee table with cocaine spread out like a deck of cards. "See what you did," he whispered in her ear and pulled the door open with her laying up against it, so he had to pull on it a couple of times before it finally opened, Gracie's small frame slid across the floor as Fielding opened the door enough for the officers to come in.

"What seems to be the problem?" One of the officers asked.

Eh, look, Fielding said , I was telling her she needs to go home. It was Officer Davis; he had recognized him from Player's Street.

The officer recognized Fielding as well, he looked over his shoulder and noticed the coke on the table. He glanced at Fielding then back to his partner.

"Eh, Martin," he said, "I got this. Check outside and make sure the neighbors stay inside their residences." Once the officer had stepped outside of the door, Officer Davis and Gracie had a silent exchange that meant you got to get out of here, now.

Fielding gave him a silent okay and let out a deep breath.

Officer Davis was a regular at Player Street and he saw him getting high, fucking, the whole nine yards. He was always doing things that were simply not becoming of an officer of the law. Fielding knew Davis would want to protect his career and his personal life.

Fielding had never run into anyone from Player Street in the daytime, what luck. What Officer Davis didn't know was that Fielding was screwing his wife too, and he didn't need to know that because right now if Fielding played his cards right, he was about to get over big time.

Davis and Fielding spoke to each other without using any words.

After a silent conversation, Officer Davis turned to Gracie and said, "Come on, Miss, you got to go, we will get you downstairs."

Gracie got up with the help of Officer Davis.

"All right now," he said to Fielding.

"Thanks, man," Fielding said.

"You fucking bastard," Gracie yelled at Fielding, realizing that the two of them knew each other. "You too, bitch," she said to Officer Davis.

The officer ignored her, "Come on let's get you home."

Fielding closed the door, not knowing that would be the last time he had seen Gracie alive.

"Fuck." he said now in his truck and pounding on the steering wheel. When he arrived at 23rd and Diamond, his guys stood outside a busted up -row home. Windows shattered. Brick to the stairs broken, crumbling. A crack house.

"Where is she?" he said to the new guy who must have been, Mark.

"Inside"

He entered. There she was on the floor he cradled her in his arms, and turned her face to his.

"Oh, Gracie," he whispered.

Her face- bloody, bruised. Lips split.

Her eyes were closed as if she was sleeping There was no mistaking that this was a dead woman.

She had clearly been beaten. The blood was all around her body, her beautiful lips that he had once kissed with such intensity were now cut and split open; she must have been punched in the face repeatedly, kicked all over. He had seen stuff like this before. They tortured her. Fielding held his feelings back. He swallowed every tear that wanted to flow from his eyes. His throat began to swell up with pure anticipation to kill whoever did this.

He asked Mark in a very low voice, "did you see anyone." Still looking down at Gracie, and getting sicker and sicker with the urge to kill.

"We found this." Mark gave Fielding a piece of paper with some letters on it. He knew exactly what it meant.

He ordered someone to call 911, and put Gracie's head gently back down on the floor and then walked to the front door. Nosey neighbors peeked from behind curtains and tried to close them quickly when he looked their way.

Too late, he saw the bastards.

Now, he had to do what he dreaded to do, what he had and hoped he would never have to face.

Jake got there in what seemed like lightning speed. Fielding didn't tell him over the phone about Gracie; he just told him to get down there quick.

Jake jumped out of his black SUV; and Fielding began walking towards him.

"What is it?" Jake demanded. Fielding didn't say anything, he tried to hold back his tears but they began coming down his face the moment he saw Jake. Jake continued to walk toward him, knowing that something had gone down but totally oblivious to what his brother was about to tell him.

"Stop. Man." Fielding stood in front of his brother but Jake barreled past him. Nothing could stop him now. Some of the guys tried to step in front of him. But still Jake pushed through them as if they were bowling pins, he mowed them down. Fielding didn't want him to see Gracie like that spread out on the floor in all that blood. In a way, he didn't want anyone to disturb her. She was very quiet right now at peace, and he wanted her to stay that way.

But no one could stop Jake, as he stumbled into the house and disappeared into the shadows. Once inside, his footsteps became dull, less demanding.

Yes, this street, this house, this room would forever be imprinted in Jake's memory, as he came to pick up his wife in the place where she took her last breath.

Jake's legs wobbled like wet noodles as if any moment he would collapse. Fielding wondered if guilt was mixed in with his grief, guilt from what Jake had put his wife through and the thought that he should have protected her, but now it was too late.

Jake breathed in deep, and his mouth dropped open heavily. Fielding saw the pain radiated throughout his brother, saw him grab at his heart and wince.

Jake shook his head as if he couldn't believe this was his wife on the floor, barely recognizable and drenched in so much blood. Wounds riddled her body.

"Oh my God," he whispered. "There's blood everywhere. We need to get her to the hospital."

He fell to his knees as paramedics and police rushed in.

"NO. NO," he screamed louder. Fielding was sure the world could hear the wails. "Don't you touch her!"

Two officers helped him up from the floor. He never got a chance to hold her. He never got a chance to touch her one more time. He would regret that for the rest of his life.

"Gracie, Gracie, Gracie,"……. he sobbed. Fielding embraced is brother.

"Come on, man, it's time to go."

Jake saw the black body bag.

"No, hell no," he yelled, "you ain't putting her in there."

"Come on man," Fielding said to him. "There is nothing we can do for her. She's gone."

"No, man." Tears streamed down Jakes face.

Fielding placed an arm around Jake and helped him out of the house. The world had just got a lot darker for them both.

At Fielding's condo, Jake looked outside at the beautiful city skyline from the balcony while enjoying a good smoke, then came back inside and asked his brother.

"You loved her right, man? He asked Fielding. "I mean it was real for you, wasn't it?"

After taking a hit from the smoke, he replied, "We both loved her."

"I don't hate you no more."

"Yeah, well good," Fielding said taking another hit.

"I should, but I don't. You're my brother."

Fielding didn't say anything, just took another hit from his brother's weed. "What the fuck you put in this?" Fielding said, taking a closer look at the tightly wrapped cigarette.

"Nothing, it's just some good weed," Jake said uninterested and knowing that Fielding was trying to change the subject.

"What we gonna fight over a dead woman now?"

"Man," Jake said, "take that back before I…"

"Before you what? You had so many chances to kill me, you ain't gonna do it now, you ain't never gonna do that shit."

"Oh, don't try me," Jake said.

"Man, we used to screw the same chicks all the time, that ain't nothin' new."

"This was different," Jake stated. "Gracie was my wife."

"And how did you show it, man? You know why I had so many chances to sleep with Gracie? Because you were out with somebody else. So, fuck you, man. I loved her, you loved her. We loved the same got damn woman, it is what it is, bro, we can't change it. No matter how mad you get, it's over, it's done, she's dead."

"You want to kill me because of that, go right ahead, because I know something is coming anyway. I see it coming. I might even deserve that shit. But what I know is when it does come it won't be you"

"Who are we, Fielding? Can you tell me that? Who are we?"

"We are brother's man, through and through. I'm down for you, you down for me. We all we got."

Fielding didn't flinch; he was ready for the fate that awaited him and one that he wasn't all too sure that he didn't deserve. Jake thought better of all his thoughts and simply said.

After a long silence, "Give me my weed, man you greedy mothafucka."

They both laughed.

Through a cloud of smoke Jake said, "I want you to move into the mansion I don't need it, I'm there by myself now." The kids are going to live with Gracie's family for a while.

"I don't want to get in your way."

"Are you kidding? You know how big that house is. You won't get in my way; Besides, it will be like old times."

"Okay, Fielding said, looking at his brother through bloodshot eyes. "Okay, man let's do it."

The next day Fielding started arranging for movers to get his stuff out of the condo and move him back into the mansion.

It was amazing he thought how he remembered all they talked about even though they were high. He wondered for a moment if Jake even remembered asking him to move in. He thought about calling him just to make sure it was okay for him to move in still.

"Hey, man," Fielding said, "you know I'm moving my stuff in, right?"

"Yeah, I know," Jake said. What's the problem?"

"No problem, just checking with you?"

"What you think, I'm that stupid."

"No, I don't think you are stupid?" I just thought you might not have remembered I mean when I was there, you never really wanted me there."

"Well, things change, don't they?" Jake tried to reassure him.

"No problem. I was just checking to make sure you remembered."

"I do, I remember everything, Fielding."

"Well good. I'll see you in a couple of hours." Fielding said, ending the call, and thinking what exactly did Jake mean by I remember everything. Something told him. This move wasn't going to be a family reunion.

.

CHAPTER SIX

CRACK

The day that Gracie died was an ordinary day. She had dropped the kids off with the baby sitter - her cousin. She liked coming back to the hood; it felt like home. She went to the corner store to pick up some cigarettes and then went five blocks just past her cousin's house and bought some crack. She had gotten hooked on the drug just a year ago. No one had even suspected it. Not even Jake who did just about everything. Gracie could have come home wearing a clown suit with big red nose, shoes and a bright orange hat and Jake wouldn't have noticed.

Fielding knew that there had been a change in Gracie and called her on it of course she denied it. It wasn't much that Fielding could do since he was getting high and Jake was getting high. They really weren't much good to themselves. Each one had their preferred drug. Fielding preferred the powder, marijuana and alcohol. Jake was into pills, marijuana, powder and boos. But Gracie had got hooked on that crack and Heroin, and she fell hard. Right after her first hit, she needed to have it again. She was one of those women who got pregnant the first time she had sex. Gracie was vulnerable like that. But the crack was her secret thing. She didn't want nobody to know especially Jake and damn sure not Fielding. Because even though Fielding would get high, he would come out of it, it was just for a limited time it was like he was in control. Jake was sloppy with his, and Gracie had fallen victim to it.

On this particular day, she decided to take her crack and smoke it with some new cats that she had seen a few days ago at this other house on Diamond Street. They had talked her into coming over there where they were at and get high. She thought why not, it was a nice night to get high and besides she liked meeting new people. She went to the house, and they laughed all the way as they walked with a crazy swagger that yelled crack head to all the unemployed people that sat on their porches watching them. But to them, they were the best thing going on. In their world, they were stepping to the beat of life, dancing to the rhythm of their own drum and that is just what Gracie wanted.

She was tired of being a mother, tired of keeping secrets and being one man's punching bag and another man's whore. No, with this thing here that she found she could be Gracie, just Gracie all day long.

So, she would ditch the grocery store which is where she was supposed to be to go to the crack house and then try to come down really quick before Jake got home.

Jake had really messed up his career. He was living off the money that Sean had left and was supposed to be helping Fielding run Tattooz Inc. but he really wasn't doing anything except hanging out all day. Gracie knew this, but she had to play along because she didn't want to fight with him.

Jake was insane with the weight gain. He was eating all the time, drinking and smoking, and gaining more weight every day. She had been tired of it for a long time but what could she do, where would she go. They had the kids.

She was in the house with two other women they were smoking when three dudes came over and said they wanted to talk to Gracie. The two girls that she had walked over with bolted out of fear. You see they knew the kids that wanted to talk to Gracie and they were known gang members in that area. Gracie didn't know them and plus she was high so when she saw them, she just giggled.

"You want to see me. What about? I must be getting popular." They picked her up from up against the wall and escorted her to a back room in the same house.

Soon as they got to the back room, they shut the door.

They began to ask her questions.

"You're Gracie Damino aren't' you?"

"Yeah, why you want to know."

"We know your husband."

"Well, if you do, then what you want from me? And your brother-in-law, Fielding."

"What about him?"

"Oh, don't worry, we know all about your affair with him."

And it was as if when they said that it struck a real nerve with Gracie almost made her snap out of her high. Now all she could think of was Fielding, him kissing her, him loving her.

The skinny guy with gold teeth was first to throw the first punch which knocked her back down to the floor. She had been used to getting punched like that so it didn't feel new to her and she sat there while she tried to get herself together and realize who was beating her up. She was punched in the chest, then kicked in the leg and another kick to the chest. Soon she felt herself drifting off into another land. The pain was alleviating from her body. She began to feel good like she could run a marathon at the end of the road, she saw Fielding he was there waiting for her. He was surrounded by a bright light and all she wanted to do now was get closer to him. She was happy because he was there. She ran closer and closer any minute now she would be in his arms. Before she could feel his loving arms around her, one last, kick and everything went black.

She never woke up.

The three young men had left the killing deed up to the young skinny guy, it was his initiation. They had been told to pick up Gracie, the wife of Jake and lover of Fielding Michaels.

They didn't know why — and they didn't ask. All they wanted was to be part of the organization; it was the only way they saw out of poverty. As ordered, they beat her. And they kept beating her — until she was dead.

Not long after Gracie was put to rest Fielding had his men, Mark and Alonzo keep their ear out in the street if they heard anything about who killed Gracie. He was sure that someone soon would be bragging about it.

Fielding was right not long after Gracie's body was found there was a posting on the internet from three young thugs who called themselves the 11th grade bandits. They were just kids Fielding thought to himself. Kids or no kids these guys wanted to be killers so they would be dealt with like killers he had no sympathy for them.

Darryl, Mark and Alonzo smoked them out, they simply waited for them one day after school. These young boys were still stupid enough to go to school. They drove an old blue Ford Escort to school every day the car must have been at least twenty years old. Mark approached them at their car asked them if they were interested in selling some drugs for him. They were interested. So, he told them to meet them later that night at the school.

The young boys, thought this was just their lucky streak first knocking off the woman for a cool $10,000.00 that they split three ways and now the drug gig, they were about to hit easy street they thought.

When Mark and Alonzo got there, they walked up to the little Ford Escort they were driving and pulled guns on them. The young boy's eyes got wide as a river.

"Get out." Mark commanded in a stern voice.

They did. One by one, the tall guy with the wide mouth and big eyes started asking questions.

"What is this man, we got money." Mark could tell he was scared but that he was trying to remain calm.

"We don't want your money." Mark said.

"No," Alonzo interrupted. "How much money do you got." He tapped Mark on the side to say go along with him.

The other two boys just stood there staring as the taller guy did all the talking.

"Look we got about $5,000.00 back at the crib. We can get it for you."

Alonzo had a look of sheer greed on his face. "Where is your crib?" He asked the tall guy.

"Not too far just a few blocks away." He pleaded.

"Okay." Alonzo said shaking his head, let's go Mark, let's go get the money and we'll let these guys go."

"But Alonzo." Mark said.

"What?" Alonzo said and then winked his eye at Mark.

Mark took this as a sign that Alonzo was bullshitting these guys.

"Okay." Mark said going along with Alonzo.

"I'll get the money with this guy" Alonzo said kicking the guy from the back in the leg. "We'll go in our car, Mark you stay here with these two knuckleheads." Alonzo said.

"Okay." Mark said thinking that they were deviating from the plan and didn't really know why because Fielding paid them well on all of their assignments. Although this one was one of the biggest assignments they ever had. Alonzo had talked about killing people in the past. Mark had only put dudes in the hospital but never killed anyone. .

Alonzo and the tall kid left in their car and Mark waited as instructed. They were gone for about twenty minutes before Alonzo and the kid came back. Alonzo had a smile on his face so he must have gotten the cash. The kid didn't especially have any kind of look on his face.

So, once they got back to the car their instructions were to call Fielding and let him know and bring them to him. He would tell them the location.

Fielding's phone rang he was at a restaurant eating with Jake they were having a meeting about the business.

"Okay meet me on the old road behind the airport, you know the one." Fielding said to Alonzo.

When he got off the phone he smiled at Jake.

"We got them." Fielding said.

"Who? The jokers that killed Gracie."

Jake was shocked. "How did they find them?"

"They were stupid enough to put their indiscretions on the internet. These young people tell on themselves all the time."

"Okay, so what now." Jake said.

"We go talk to them, see who set this whole thing up." Fielding said.

Fielding motioned for the check and Jake took in a deep sigh of relief as they got ready to go.

Fielding and Jake both rode together in Fielding's truck to the back road behind the airport, Fielding had met plenty of his guys back here for clandestine meetings in the past.

They were sitting in the truck when Alonzo pulled up with the tall kid and Mark followed behind riding in the small Escort with the other two guys. They kept guns on both of them while they had one of the boys drive the car.

When they saw Fielding and Jake, Mark ushered the boys from the vehicles.

Fielding said to the tall kid with Alonzo once he was standing in front of him.

"You know the girl who you killed?"

The tall kid shook his head no.

"That was my brother's wife." Fielding turned to Jake. "He is real fucked up right now."

Fielding leaned in to him. "So am I."

Fielding looked at these young kids they had a look on their face realizing that they were in deep shit. Fielding noticed one kid begin to have a wet line of piss flow down the leg of his pants.

"Yeah, this is a bad thing." Fielding said to the boys watching as he interrogated the other kid.

"Who set you dudes up to do this hit."

"We don't know, the kid standing next to the one who just peed himself confessed. "We never met him." He now had tears streaming down his face. Fielding looked over at Alonzo and told him to watch the tall kid while he went to talk to the other little guy.

"No, well you must have had contact with someone. Who was that?"

"I don't know, some guy. Tall, big black guy, he just said he was looking for someone to do a job for him and told us that it would be like an initiation type thing and if we did it, he would pay us and then call us again for more work if it came around."

"Why you wanna do work like this?" Fielding asked.

"Why you do work like this?" The tall kid said.

Fielding turned around. "Your right kid, I probably wasn't much older than you when I started in this business and you know what it is a game of Russian roulette every day you never know when you gonna get popped."

"So, who sent you to kill that lady?" Fielding asked again.

"We only know the guy who gave us the dough and told us where to meet her and what to do."

Fielding was tired of talking to these dudes. He took pulled out his gun and pointed it at the tall kid.

"But we gave him the money."

"Who, what money?" Fielding said. "The money from the hit, this guy over here asked us for some money we gave it to him." Fielding shook his head at Alonzo. "Doesn't matter, you are still going to die tonight son, you made a deal with the wrong man. He ain't in charge." Fielding pulled the trigger and the bullet made a nice hole in the boy's heart he fell backwards on the ground dead.

The other two boys started crying and pleading for their lives. Fielding shot them both quickly he couldn't take their pleading anymore.

Then he began chastising Alonzo about the money.

"You making side deals now."

"Know I just figured I could get the money since they had it, you know kill two birds with…" Fielding cut him off.

"Let me do the thinking around here," Fielding said. "Next time I send you out to do a job stick to the plan don't deviate. Now, where is the money?" Fielding said.

Alonzo went over to the car and came back with an envelope. He snatched the envelope from Alonzo and looked the money over, good you can keep it, that was the same thing I was going to give you." Fielding said and shoved the envelope back at him.

Alonzo and Mark were instructed to put the bodies of the three boys back into their Escort and set it on fire. They drove it further out into the swampy area on the back road. It would be weeks before they found them.

When Fielding and Jake got back into the truck Fielding noticed how quiet Jake had been during the whole ordeal.

"You okay man?" Fielding asked.

"Yeah, I'm fine. It's just that we really didn't find out anything. I mean don't get me wrong I'm glad we caught those dudes they were just going to grow up to be thug killers anyway in a sense we did society a favor tonight but we still hit a dead end. We still don't know who hired the hit on Gracie."

"I know." Fielding said.

"It makes us vulnerable." Jake said, "Not knowing who our enemies are."

"Don't worry about that Jake, trust me we will find out who did this even if it takes my last breath." Fielding said.

About a month later there was a story on the news about three young teenagers found dead in a car that had been set on fire.

Fielding didn't even flinch when he heard it, while getting out the shower. He finished getting dressed and started on with his day. Another day another dollar Fielding thought this was his life. He had a therapy session today and he couldn't wait to talk to his new therapist.

CHAPTER SEVEN

A NEW THERAPIST

Now that Gracie had been murdered Fielding really thought it was time for him to talk to someone about his issues. He was dealing with a lot of grief. He wanted to see his son and these back- to- back deaths were really making him depressed. He found a therapist on line and gave the guy a call. He told him to come in so they could have a session and Fielding could decide if he wanted to come back if he felt that he was getting the help he needed.

"Hello Fielding?"

"How are you nice to meet you?"

"I'm Mr. Kincaid. You want to tell me a little bit about why you came in today."

"Yeah, well, I'm trying to kick the smoking and drinking. Meanwhile I just had another death in the family and I feel like perhaps I need some grief therapy as well."

"Great, well that is what I am here for. I'm sorry for your loss, Fielding. Can you tell me about the recent death."

"It was my brother's wife."

"Your sister-in-law?"

"Yeah," Fielding answered, wincing at the term. He hated hearing Gracie referred to that way. "My brother and I even picked out flowers together. "That's what that dream was about." Fielding said out loud to himself.

"What did you say?"

"Oh, nothing it was just that I had a dream before Gracie's died, and now it makes sense."

"You think you had a premonition of your sister-in-law's death."

"Do you have to keep saying that?"

"Saying what?" The man said.

"Calling Gracie my sister-in-law. I know who she was."

The therapist leaned back in his chair. "Okay" "Go on Fielding. Tell me about your dream."

"I had a dream. In retrospect, it was a warning. Someone was going to die. I just didn't know it would be Gracie.

"How are you coping?"

"I'm managing."

"And your brother?"

"He's coping too, better than I thought."

"What kind of relationship do you have with your brother?"

"What do you mean?"

"Do you get along?"

"Sure, we get along , for years we would even share the same women, have group sex with women."

"Do you still do that?"

"We slowed down a little, but every now and then we call up some girls." Fielding said matter of factly.

"You and your brother have sex together."

"Yeah, but not with each other. Just the same room, different girls. You interested?"

"No," Mr. Kincaid answered.

"No, I think we hit on something here." Fielding said now taking on the role of the therapist, and not letting him off the hook that he caught him on. Fielding looked at the therapist and then got a wry looking on his face and said "She not satisfying you, is she?"

"Who?"

"Your wife."

The therapist sighed, and looked down at his wedding ring. "You're kidding. I don't get it at all." He confessed.

"I can help you out with that," Fielding took his phone out of his pocket and began dialing.

"What are you doing" Mr. Kincaid defended his thoughts.

"Don't deprive yourself man, I can get somebody over here right now," Fielding put his hand up to Mr. Kincaid and told him to hold on. He began talking in the phone, "Yo, where is Kitty, oh yeah, tell her to get up and dressed and get over to… hold on…what's the address here?" He said to Mr. Kincaid.

"You can't -."

"Look, don't worry about it, it is on me." Fielding said ignoring what the therapist was saying, he knew full well that the solicitation of prostitution in this manner was illegal but he didn't care. "What's the address here?"

Mr. Kincaid began telling him, "3492 Walkers Ave. but" what was he saying, he thought after the address fell out of his mouth. This man, Fielding what was he doing to him, he felt as if he was being seduced.

"Okay," he said into the phone, "she'll be here in about twenty." Fielding said looking at his therapist.

"Minutes." Mr. Kincaid choked on his words.

"Yeah, she'll be here in twenty minutes, that's the fastest I can do."

"No, I don't mean it like that," the man began to raise his voice and then when he saw he was getting a little too aggressive he calmed down. "Fielding you can't do that." Mr. Kincaid chastised.

"Can't do what, can't do a favor for my therapist. As much as you help me out, listening to my problems the least I can do is hook you up. You gave me the address, you know why, because you want it man and there is nothing wrong with that." Mr. Kincaid was a short man, he was bald, looked about 45, wore glasses and dressed like he had been dressing that way since the fourth grade. No style at all. "All my ladies are clean man they all use protection and are tested on a regular basis."

"But…"

Fielding looked at his therapist, seeing that this white man, was feeling a bit embarrassed because he knew the truth which was that he really wanted Kitty to come over to the office and do whatever she was good at doing. He was getting excited thinking about it.

Fielding could tell he wanted it. He just needed a little push and reassurance that everything would be discreet.

"It's okay, nobody will know. You good?" Fielding said, and walked over to the window and looked out. "There she is now."

Within moments Kitty was knocking on the door. She walked in and Mr. Kincaid had no idea what to do when he saw those long legs. He reacted as if a man who had too much to drink, he began rubbing his thighs with his hands over and over again. Kitty wore a weave in her hair making her hair extremely long.

Fielding smiled when Kitty came to the door "Mr. Kincaid is a little shy why don't you go over and say hi." He pushed her a little towards Mr. Kincaid and then tapped her butt. "Serve him, well." He whispered in her ear and sent her on her way.

He winked at Mr. Kincaid, "Have fun."

He walked out and stopped at the white SUV that was outside. He walked up to the driver side of the vehicle. A young light skin dude was driving the car. "Wait for her."

"Okay, boss."

"She'll be fine. He's new." Call me when she comes out just hit me up 411, Fielding had codes for everything. That meant that everything was cool. He left the SUV and got into his own ride. He now had the therapist in his back pocket and that was exactly where he wanted him.

CHAPTER EIGHT

PAST LOVERS

After a few more months of therapy and attempts to slow down his drug and alcohol use Fielding was starting to find a smoother path to get to day 23. He would get to day12 or 13 without a drink or a smoke, mess up and start again from day one. Still progress was progress. The money was flowing in steadily at the record label with no discrepancies this month, but after Alonzo's stunt with the young boys' payoff, Fielding remained hyper – vigilant. Then fall back and have to start all over again from day one to break his bad habit. He would continue to keep a close eye, especially since that stunt that Alonzo pulled with the

Young boys' payoff. Fielding remained hyper-vigilant.

***

The weather forecast predicted a storm. The storm blew in Fielding's estranged wife.

Fielding hadn't realized how much he missed her until he seen her. Her long, sleek red hair fell down her back, and she wore black form -fitting pants, a crisp white shirt, and a short white jacket with fur on the lapels. Taupe boots showed off just enough of her legs to remind Fielding of everything he had been missing.

He stood by his car, suddenly aware of the shell he'd become without her. The drugs, the women, the drinking- distractions. Nothing else.

They met in the street. When she stepped out of her car and walked toward him, he wrapped her in his arms. For a moment, he felt whole.

But still he wondered what had brought her back to town?

He felt like now he had his life back. This was the best high he ever felt. Holding her close to his body. At the same time, she was the one thing that he feared the most. Laurel was the woman who made him vulnerable.

"Why didn't you tell me that you were coming?" He spoke.

"Because you know what we got."

"I know. That thing that people look for, all their lives, we got that." Fielding said.

She laughed and tugged at his shirt. "Where is my tattoo, did you remove it?"

"Are you kidding?" It is still there on my shoulder, you'll see later.

She grinned.

"What you got to show me." He said, looking at her crouch.

"You are so nasty."

They walked back to the car.

"You like it." he said, now pressing her back up against the car and sliding his hand into her pants. As the rain began to fall, he kissed her. Fingers stroking her, he made her come again leaning on the side of the car in the street. started to push up on her against the car.

"Come on, let's get out of here." She said, breathless. Realizing what had just happened and that no other man could ever command her like that. This man had a magic spell over her that she knew she couldn't shake. She loved the feeling but it consumed her and that made her very afraid.

Back at the mansion, Fielding led her to the bedroom. It was nothing like his condo- this was his sanctuary. He undressed her slowly, reverently, kissing her, savoring her.

She melted in him.

He kissed her belly, her thighs, sucking softly, biting gently, teasing her until she couldn't take it anymore. Then he lifted her, carried her to the bed he went down on her, she transitioned. He held her while her body shook, uncontrollably. He made love until they both collapsed in peace.

"While she was basking in Fielding's love making, she asked him. "Why"

"Why what?" Fielding said as they lay in bed together sharing a pillow.

"You know."

"I don't know." Fielding said.

"You know." Laurel said, biting her lip half way and looking at her lover.

"Because you taste like chicken and waffles." Fielding laughed. With this sweet, sweet syrup drizzled all over you.

Laurel's body began to shiver just by the way this man was talking to her about how her body felt in his mouth.

The dirty conversation was making her feel closer to her man as he told her his intimate feelings about making love to her.

"I love every inch of your body." He said, then he kissed her.

"I love sucking you." Then he kissed her.

"I love licking you." Then he kissed her again.

"I love fucking you." Then he kissed her again and with that he placed his fingers on her vagina and began to massage her and she began to feel like she couldn't breathe just from the touch of his hands.

She couldn't control her body as it did what he commanded it to do.

When she came with just his fingers again, she then got on top of him she guided his huge third leg inside of her and immediately began to grind on him and they did it together eventually climaxing as one.

When morning came Fielding woke up and smoked a cigarette although he was steady saying in his head this would be his last.

"I thought you were quitting. Laurel said.

"I am. This is my last one. "

"Where's my coffee?" Fielding said turning around and looking her body up and down still feeling very horny.

She turned around and ran to the kitchen to start a pot of coffee brewing. She came back in ten minutes with a cup of hot coffee. He took the cup from her and placed it on the banister of the terrace.

He grabbed her up in his arms and put her on his lap.

"I was missing you." He said and kissed her.

"I was missing you too." Laurel said.

"You know you came back at the wrong time."

Laurel pulled back from his grip and asked "What do you mean?"

"Laurel we are in the middle of a war, some real bad shit is going down, you got to go, I don't want you here right now, it's too dangerous."

"We are in this together." Laurel said.

"I'm not going to risk your life. You can't stay I'm putting you on a plane tomorrow."

"No," Laurel argued. "I'm staying, it's been too long since we've been together."

"If you stay here, you are going get hurt." Fielding said.

"Then get out." Laurel got up off her man's lap and went over to her luggage and started taking clothes out to indicate that she wasn't going anywhere.

"Get out of what?" Fielding asked.

"Out of the game." Laurel commanded.

Fielding looked at her. "You know they killed Gracie."

"I heard about her death." Laurel said not knowing how to really feel about the news.

"Not just a death honey, murder. Someone murdered her." Fielding corrected.

"Who?" Laurel said.

"I don't know who is behind it. But the young boys who actually pulled the trigger are history." Fielding confirmed.

"Fielding, you didn't…" Laurel said.

"I had to, they were headed down the wrong road they would have just done the same thing to someone else and eventually they were going to end up dead anyway."

"Yeah, but that is not for you to decide."

"Well, I did." Fielding said. "Let's change the subject, babe, I am not proud of what I did I never am, God will deal with me." Fielding said.

And with that the conversation ended.

***

They left the mansion that night and went out to a spot where Fielding often went to practice shooting his gun. He needed to make sure his shot was good because he just had a feeling that he was going to need his skills to be sharper than ever. It was dark out now but it was perfect to practice. They found a place at the creek. It had a dark eerie energy- rumors of bodies buried there from years ago. Murdered by a serial killer and the place still had the feel of their deaths in the trees. Laurel felt uncomfortable as they drove up into the grass and Fielding gave her the history of the area. Fielding knew a way inside where the car would be okay, he didn't want to leave it on the street and alert any police officers. Besides they could use the light from the car. They got out the car. Laurel looked at him like she didn't want to go.

The smell of the wet grass took Fielding back to when he was just a kid running through the park in Florida after it rained. It intrigued him it filled him with the right amount of nostalgia for the moment.

"What's wrong?"

"I don't know if we should go in there."

"I think we should" Fielding confirmed, and put out his hand.

"It's getting dark."

"It's perfect," he said smiling. "Besides the lights from the car, is just enough for us."

Fielding pulled out a cigarette as they walked and lit it up and began to smoke. He found some empty bottles as they walked and gathered them up in his arms. When they got to the spot that Fielding was looking for, he told Laurel to wait where she was a few feet away from where he was going to set up the bottles. He set them up on a sturdy rock the rest he put beside it then started to walk back towards her. When he got close to her, he pulled a pistol out from the back of his pants turned around quickly and shot off a few rounds into the empty bottles of beer that he set up. One by one the glass splattered into the air. Laurel jumped at every pop sound of the gun. When he finished, he turned around and looked at her with the cigarette still in his mouth. Then went and set some more bottles up on the rock. You could tell by his movements that he was enjoying this.

He walked back over to her "Que" He said to her in Spanish. "Miedo de el sonido de una pistola"

"What?" She said not understanding what he just said in Spanish.

"Exactly." Fielding said.

He got closer to her. "Why you shaking?" He got behind her and put his arms around her held her close then took the gun from behind him again this time he put it in her hands and said softly in her ear "now, aim, squeeze and shoot that moootheeerfuuuuccccka." He commanded and she wet her panties instantly by the sound of his sultry voice in her ear. The bullets began to fly out of the gun towards the bottles, the glass shattered as if plucked over by someone's finger.

They practiced for a couple of hours. Laurel was a good aim, but Fielding needed to feel a little more comfortable with her behind the weapon. So, they practiced for another hour. When they finished Fielding felt like she was on her way to becoming a professional. And he was satisfied.

The next day they did it again. Every day Laurel was getting better aim, better focus. She was beginning to understand the weapon and not fear it. He was pleased.

Fielding lit up a cigarette, "What day did you say this was?" Laurel watched as he smoked like he was not even thinking about quitting.

"Technically it is still day 20, "okay then cigarette comes out." She slid the cigarette out from between Fielding's lips.

Fielding allowed her to do it.

"Day 20." Fielding confirmed gazing at his woman. She was allowing him to cheat by starting at Day 20 instead of starting all over again.

Day 20 wasn't that hard for him. He wasn't craving the nicotine as much but needed to chew on something so he began chewing on a straw. It wasn't the sexiest thing in the world but for the time being it worked for him. Laurel pretended not to notice.

They went to the market to pick up some groceries. Fielding played with her the whole time up and down the aisles. They went grocery shopping together, playing like newlyweds. Then they ran into Miss Mary.

Fielding couldn't dodge her. She stood directly in front of them.

Miss Mary wore glasses, and a skirt that came down to her knees and some flat shoes. She truly looked like a school teacher right out of a classic novel.

"Hi you doing, Miss Mary." Fielding said feeling very awkward right now.

"Hi, Fielding." Miss Mary said to Fielding but looking Laurel up and down.

"I thought I'd hear from you by now." Miss Mary said.

"I know, some things came up." Fielding said.

"I see." She looked Laurel up and down again."

"Miss Mary," he began awkwardly. He truly did like Miss Mary; she was a very nice woman and the sex wasn't bad at all. He needed to come clean not only in front of his wife but for Miss Mary as well. "This is my wife, Laurel. Laurel this is Miss Mary, she was helping me quit smoking."

"Hi, nice to meet you." Laurel said, already getting the picture that something more had gone on.

But to Fielding's surprise, Miss Mary did not say hello to Laurel instead she addressed Fielding again. "I didn't know that you were married, that was something that you forgot to tell me."

When she did that, Fielding decided it would be best if they talked alone.

"Excuse me for a minute Laurel, go head finish shopping, I'll meet you outside."

Fielding shuffled Miss Mary outside. When they got outside, he took her over to her car.

"What are you doing?" Fielding said when they got outside.

"I thought we had something." She spoke.

"We did. We had that one night together. Hey look I didn't know she was coming back, and you have a husband, she caught me off guard. She is my wife. I love her."

"But we can still have something. That bastard I am married to…" Miss Mary said, putting her hands on Fielding's chest.

He pulled her hands down and held them together as if she were in handcuffs. "I can't see you anymore. That's done."

"Bastard." Miss Mary snapped and stormed off.

Laurel came out a few minutes later with a cart that had a few bags in it. When Fielding saw her, he helped put the groceries in the car. When they started to drive off, Laurel asked about Miss Mary.

"Is she okay?"

"Yeah, she is going to be fine."

"You know it is simply incredible that, I have to endure other women that you are apparently sleeping with and who have no problem approaching you in public. Who is she?"

"Don't do that."

"Do what?"

"Don't question me when you have your own secrets."

Laurel sat back against the car seat and exhaled. She had nothing more to say.

They drove the rest of the way home in silence.

CHAPTER NINE

DAY 21

It was getting harder and harder without Miss Mary helping him with the smoking habit and without Mr. Kincaid whom Fielding had turned into a client. What had become even harder was sleeping with one woman. He had to admit that when Laurel wasn't around, he was having a ball. He and Jake were getting laid on a regular. They were partying hard and now all of that came to a screeching halt. The one thing he did not want was for Laurel to leave him again. He had to be a faithful, dutiful husband now.

The coke was gone, the alcohol under control. But the sex and the cigarettes – were still real vices.

Jake hadn't changed. Still on coke, still partying, still refusing responsibility. The kids were okay, but no doubt missing their father and at the same time mourning their mother.

Jake had a new girl he liked, but he wasn't looking to settle down.

Fielding still continued to go to therapy to see Dr. Kincaid but he was so hooked on Kitty he didn't even bother with Fielding's troubles anymore. Now whenever Fielding went to therapy Dr. Kincaid would pay him instead of the other way around.

Addictions were hard to break Fielding was seeing first hand. He realized that a huge part of it was that a person really had to want to stop. That was the question did he really want to stop the lifestyle that he had built for himself. Did he want to stop having sex with women who were not his wife?

Day 22

Laurels 30th birthday.

Fielding had never been the romantic type, but Gracie's death reminded him to cherish the living. He filled the house with red roses Twenty dozen, in fact. Rose petals lined the bedroom floor. A diamond ring sparkled under the candlelight.

Laurel came home and gasped.

Laurel was turning 30. She was a few years older than Fielding. When she saw all those roses and a beautiful new diamond ring t she was overwhelmed with happiness.

She hadn't thought much about herself she was missing her son. Today she had done some shopping for some new clothes and some clothes to send down to the baby. Fielding hadn't even seen him yet. He finally knew about him but hadn't held his own child yet.

Fielding had a beautiful dinner catered that was already waiting in the dining room. The table was exquisitely decorated with a red table cloth and candles beautiful wine glasses adorned the table. They had a delicious meal of shrimp scampi and lobster tail. They talked about old times, when they first met when Fielding had been pushed out of the window by his father.

How a father could do that Laurel still didn't understand. It was because of that horrible incident that they met. She had become Fielding's live in nurse, his life line.

"I want to bring the baby here." Laurel said.

"Of course, I want him here with us." Fielding said, "I haven't even seen my son yet."

"I wanted to make sure that it would be okay to bring him that is why I left him in Florida."

"I understand, look I want you to take your time it has been a long time let's do this right."

"Okay," Laurel said smiling." When can we get him?"

"We can get him now. Let's call and get the nanny and him here as soon as tomorrow." Fielding said.

After they finished their meal Fielding and his beautiful wife finished off the night dancing alone. Fielding had decided to go back to the condo to have the intimate dinner. Besides in the condo they had the backdrop of the lights of the city from every office building downtown shining on them as they held each other and danced to My funny Valentine by Etta James that had now become Fielding's favorite song. He had heard many versions of the song from Chaka Khan to old blue eyes himself, but no one hit those notes like Etta James it was as if she were a one-woman symphony.

His heart was changing all he could see in the whole wide world even though now he held her close to him and they danced around the room as if old lost lovers. And still as he held the woman that he loved he thought about the woman he knew first, before all other women his mother and how he missed her. Then he thought of Gracie and their world they created that was never quite right yet and now no longer existed.

Fielding grew more excited about his son coming to Philadelphia as he began to get comfortable with the idea. Finally, Spencer would be here with him to complete the family.

Spencer arrived the next day. Spencer was two years old now so he was walking and saying some words. When Fielding saw him coming towards him at the airport, he couldn't help but break out in a wide grin.

His nanny was behind him telling him to go to his daddy.

The closer Spencer got to him he saw that he had those same beautiful eyes that had been passed down from his mother, his real mother, Chill. His son now would carry the trait. He feared what other trait had his son received from his lineage. Was he anything like his grandfather, his father Sean Damino? What kind of man would young Spencer be? It was all too soon to think of that now Fielding began to think he was just a baby and immediately he loved him.

He picked him up in his arms and said hello.

Young Spencer said "Hi Daddy."

That's right I'm your daddy I'm so glad to meet you. I'm sorry it has taken so long for us to meet but I promise we will stay together.

Young Spencer put his head on his father's shoulder. Laurel thought she might cry but held back many tears. The nanny just stood and watched waiting for her next cue.

Laurel introduced the nanny to her husband. "This is Abby."

"Hi." Fielding said taking a glance of her. She was a short Latino woman. She was older than both Laurel and Fielding. She looked like she was a good person to take care of Spencer just from first glances.

"It is nice to meet you." Abby said sounding as if she had prac-ticed that line for quite some time.

"It's nice to meet you too." Fielding said and then gave Laurel a funny look. Laurel tried to ignore her husband being rude. But instead shot him a look that she would have given young Spencer for doing something that he wasn't supposed to.

Fielding patted him on the back and then looked at the women and said "Let's go".

So, they went out to retrieve the car and drove to the mansion. The nanny was in awe when she saw the huge home. The house they had in Florida was nice but it was not as big as this. Her eyes were filled with excitement of living in such a place.

"Your quarters are downstairs, Abby, Fielding said to the nanny.

Abby had a beautiful room just off the kitchen. It used to be the cook's old room. But they were not there anymore now since things had changed with Sean's death Jake had gotten rid of all the old staff saying that he wanted to start over.

Young Spencer's room was not far from his parents. His room was connected by theirs's by an interior door.

When Jake came home that night, he was excited to meet his little nephew. He played with him for a long time before tiring him out. Laurel gave him to Abby to feed him and then it was off to bed.

Fielding was so happy to have his family with him under one roof he never thought this would happen. Young Spencer had a head full of curly hair and a smile that was infectious.

Laurel kept Young Spencer dressed in the cutest clothes always some kind of sports paraphernalia. She hoped he would grow up to be like his dad a business man or either his uncle and become a professional ball player. Fielding would say this is my young doctor. He wanted Spencer to become something totally different than he was and not follow in the family footsteps at all. He didn't wish that curse on him. He did not want a gangster son.

Fielding spent so much time with Young Spencer, Laurel couldn't believe it. He would play with him in the morning in his room with his cars and carry him piggy back everywhere.

Laurel warned him he was spoiling him.

"I know I want to spoil him" Fielding would say and threw him up in the air and caught him. "I want him to have whatever he wants."

Spencer laughed as his father caught him and then rolled him down the ground acting as if he were going to fall. Young Spencer felt no worries when his father played with him, he knew he was in safe hands.

This went on for weeks Fielding was falling in love with Young Spencer. Young Spencer was falling in love with his dad.

That night, Laurel curled up beside Fielding, after putting Young Spencer to bed.

"You are so good with Spencer." Laurel said, laying on Fielding's chest.

"I hope so, that's my baby I'm supposed to be good with him." Fielding said.

"I know but it's just I never seen this side of you, the daddy side." Laurel said.

"Well now you do." Fielding said.

"While you were away from me what did you do Laurel?" Fielding asked.

"What do you mean?" Laurel said feeling that the conversation was taking a drastic turn.

"You know how did you hold out on sex for so long or did you?" Fielding asked.

"It was hard." Laurel said beginning to feel a bit uneasy with the conversation because there were some things that her husband did not know and she prayed that he would never find out.

"Were you seeing anyone in Florida?" Fielding asked.

"No." Laurel said as if she were insulted. "I could never do that."

"You can tell me baby; I'd rather hear it from you then some-place else." Fielding said.

"Well, no, the answer is no." Laurel said. "You don't see me tripping over Miss Mary, do you?"

"I told you that didn't mean anything, just a fluke."

"Okay, I get it. and I was taking care of our son. I was trying to get over you,"

"And did you?"

"Did I what?"

"Get over me."

"No."

"Good, let's leave that right there and just enjoy being in each other's arms again."

But something in Fielding's gut told him she wasn't being entirely honest. And the feeling lingered.

CHAPTER TEN

CHEATERS

Fielding was growing more confident in his ability to stay clean. He hung in there for the rest of the 22 days without slipping, and that wasn't easy. Yeah, he might have cheated a little but, he felt that he was steady.

The next day Fielding left Laurel sleeping in the bed. The clouds outside were an angry gray color, they were expecting a rain storm. He was up early still thinking about last night's conversation. Fielding always had a suspicious mind and he had gone through his wife's belongings and found her check book the night before. There were some pretty hefty checks she had written out to a man named Benjamin Castor. He was hoping that she would come clean with it the first night. He hoped whatever it was she was hiding from him she would tell it. To his dismay she didn't. He called his friend , a private investigator named Jamal.

"Hey Jamal, how are you?" Fielding said into his cell phone.

"I'm okay man, what's up?" Jamal retorted.

"I need you to do some work for me I need you to find out all you can about a man named Benjamin Castor."

"Benjamin Castor, okay I got it. What's up anything specific you want me to look for." Jamal said.

"Yeah, you can start with if he knew my wife in Florida whatever you can find out about him will be helpful. And Jamal, make it as quick as possible." Fielding added.

"Not a problem," Jamal responded.

Jamal got back to Fielding in three days with some information. It was exactly what Fielding was looking for he just wasn't sure how much Fielding was going to like what he found. But his job wasn't to worry about that, his job was to report back the information.

That night Laurel had planned a romantic dinner with wine, blackened salmon, asparagus, and mashed potatoes with chives. For dessert, she had a delicious strawberry cheese cake she had ordered from the local bakery. She found a playlist with soft love songs to play while they ate their dinner. Young Spencer was with the nanny on the other wing of the mansion for the evening so they would have privacy.

Fielding found it difficult to eat his meal when he had a burning question on his mind. So halfway through his dinner he dropped his fork down on his plate and asked Laurel.

"Who was he?"

Laurel had a dumb look on her face. "Who was who?" She asked digging into the mashed potatoes then placing it in her mouth.

Fielding got up from his seat and walked over to the desk just behind the dining room table and pulled a white envelope off of the top of the table. He sat down calmly at the table and opened up the envelope and began showing his wife receipts for large amounts of money every month for one year.

"1,000, 1,500, 2,500."

Laurel began to get up from her seat. Fielding grabbed her by the arm. " Uhh, uhh," he said his strength prevented her from getting up. " Look, he went through some more checks on the table, it gets better, 5,000, 7,500" Who is he?"

"I can explain," Laurel confessed.

"Oh, so now you can explain," Fielding said. "Well please do. Because that money that you wrote checks on was my money, Laurel. Now I am going to ask you again. Who is he? Take your time."

"Nobody."

" Oh yeah," Fielding said. "Well, nobody has a criminal record as long as my arm, three kids, and a wife in Augusta Georgia, and my money" Fielding said.

Laurel's entire mode changed within an instant and she began to yell intensely at her husband "I was so mad at you… You liar…" Laurel spat. "You were still sleeping with Gracie and you acted like nothing was going on." Laurel's words now hit him like punches to his stomach. "You married me based on lies and we said we were going to be truthful to each other. Do you remember that?"

"No, I'm not going to let you do this, this is not about me, Laurel you did this." He pointed at her then pushed his chair back with force and stood up from the table. And then without any warning at all, he took his right arm and brushed over all of the dishes and glasses on his side of the table clean, his plate of salmon and potatoes hit the floor the glass of wine splattered against the wall and broke.

"Who is he to you Laurel?" Fielding said again. Laurel got up worried about what Fielding would do next. She began stepping back slowly away from the table. She had been so thankful that she hadn't put candles as a centerpiece as she had thought to do if so, the whole house would be going up in flames. She saw the fury in his eyes and it scared her. She had never been afraid of her husband before but now he had a look on his face that proved to her that he was a very dangerous man. She continued to step back from Fielding until she bumped up against the wall.

She decided in a split second that she needed to tell him the truth no matter how much it hurt. Not even if this meant the end of her marriage.

She began.

"I met him one night I don't know what I was thinking." Then in the middle of the story, she stopped looking for the words to continue.

"Yeah, okay, what? You were fucking this guy?"

"You weren't there." She shouted.

He shouted back at her, "Because you didn't want me there." He lowered his voice and regained his composure. "So, what you were fucking this guy and what happened?"

"He threatened to come up and tell you everything if I didn't give him money, so I did, but then the amount kept getting bigger and bigger and before I knew it, I realized what I had gotten mixed up in."

"Where did you meet him?"

"Coming out of the gym one day."

"Yeah, I had a babysitter and I wanted to lose some of the baby weight. I'd go in and use the bike. One day I came out and he was just… there."

"Just there huh."

"Yeah. In fact, that was the first time I noticed him. He said hello to me then the next time I saw him he asked if I wanted to have lunch sometime and then, from there, it just happened."

"Okay so let me get this straight you met this guy who happened to just be there outside of the gym that you were going to to lose baby fat. You go out to dinner with him, have sex, and the next thing you know you are the target of an extortion scam. Really. He set you up, Laurel. Don't you know that people know who you are? Word gets around we don't need to be on the news. The streets talk, babe" Fielding grabbed her neck from the back, in his hand with a fist full of hair entwined in his grasp. He didn't want to hurt her but he could feel his anger filling up in his bones. He had never hurt Laurel but right now she had pushed him to a limit that he had to use all of his strength to let it go.

"Uhm" Fielding let out a grimacing sound. He gave her a look of disappointment and let her go and stepped away from her and the wall.

Thankful that he let her go she put her hand around her neck to massage the pain out. Then she forgot her fear and got angry "What are you looking at me like that for? Your slate ain't clean. You are a hypocrite."

"Yeah well, you know what you know." Fielding said stepping closer to his wife and when he was close enough to her again, he began to whisper in her ear "When yawl females gonna realize that you ain't men, you can't do what we do. In the end, you just end up getting fucked ."

His words penetrated her spirit and she felt imprudent. She knew he was right. She had heard that saying from her own mother when she was a little girl. A man can get down in the mud with the pigs and roll around in it all day and still get up Mr. So and So. A woman can get down in that same muddy hole and crawl out a whore every time.

Slow hot tears began to run down Laurel's face.

"What you crying for?"

"I'm sorry."

"Yeah, I know you are, you keep your mouth shut about this, you understand, don't say anything to anyone until I can make this all go away." Fielding stepped back from her so that he could look at her face to face again.

"Fielding I'm sorry," Laurel said reaching a hand out to her husband.

Fielding pretended not to see it "Don't worry about it. Go on upstairs" he instructed. "I'll meet you up there in a minute." While Laurel was upstairs Fielding made a phone call.

He was calling Jamal who was on standby waiting for this call from Fielding. "Yeah, how's he feeling."

"Not too good he's probably going to need about twenty to thirty stitches, some new teeth, and a wheelchair."

---

36 hours before

Fielding received a phone call from Jamal earlier . Jamal was an inquisitive dude and he had continued to do some research on the man that had been blackmailing Fielding's wife Benjamin Castor and it was something that just didn't add up to him at all.

Jamal reported that while Laurel was living in a gated community in Florida and didn't go out much except to exercise at the local gym and to the movies every now and then so how did Benjamin know her. After he did a little more digging, he found a list of phone numbers that Benjamin had been calling in Philadelphia. He had made many calls to Philadelphia monthly. His wife and kids were in Georgia. He had gotten locked up in South Carolina when he was caught speeding with drugs on his person. He was just a bad dude all around. What Jamal found out he had to let Fielding know right away. He knew that this would not sit well.

After being satisfied with what he heard, Fielding commanded for Jamal to let him go. He hung up the phone then he started up the stairs.

Jamal was a huge guy at least 6'6" and did not miss a meal. He weighed at least 300 pounds. Jamal was a great investigator but an even better bouncer, which is what he used to do before working his own business . He had found Benjamin Castor at a local bar in Opa Locka Florida. He was having a blast drinking with a few buddies as they flirted with some women buying them drinks laughing and feeling on their thighs if they let them. He had the poor soul tied up in a basement now for three days waiting to hear from his boss with instructions on what to do with him. He watched as Jamal ate in front of him. Talked on the phone about his impending demise and every now and then he went over to him and gave a punch in the face.

Benjamin Castor's face was beginning to look like mush. He was tied up in a chair and right now he looked like neither a lover nor an extortionist. He now had a swollen eye, a busted lip, and countless cuts and bruises all over his body from the beating of a baseball bat that Jamal had taken to him when he picked him up from the bar. Benjamin didn't come quietly so Jamal had to work him over. He was pretty sure that both his knee caps were broken. But at this point, he was so delirious and pretty sure he was going to die all he could do now was laugh hysterically.

Jamal cut him loose and dragged him up the basement stairs of the old abandoned house. He opened up the back door and threw him out with the rest of the trash. Benjamin hit the cement with a thud. Jamal left out from the back of the house and walked around to the front got in his car and drove off. He called Fielding back and reported to him. "It's done."

Fielding hung up the phone. Laurel was just getting out of the shower. Fielding stepped into the room Laurel didn't hear him come in as she concentrated on drying her body and hair. Fielding walked up behind her, startling her.

"Fielding, I didn't hear you," Laurel said startled by her husband.

Fielding didn't respond, he felt so much anger for his wife right now. He turned her around so now she was facing him. She looked at him not knowing what he was going to do next but she knew he was angry. She could tell by the way he was now holding her. His grip was tight.

"I have a problem with another man touching you."

Laurel said nothing. She didn't know what to say. She felt that if she pleaded with him, he wouldn't like that, and if she defended herself again this time the fight would be worse.

He began kissing her but it wasn't the kind of kiss a man gives to a woman whom he loves. This was more like a vindictive kiss. He placed his hands on her neck and what began as caressing had changed into a stronghold on her shoulders.

"Fielding" Laurel yelled out.

But he continued to hold her shoulders tighter and began unbuttoning his pants quickly as he had her pinned against the wall.

"Stop"

Laurel yelled out, tears beginning to stream down her cheeks.

Fielding ignored her as he pressed up against her body with force and just as quickly as it all had started, he stopped. He pulled himself back from a place he knew he could never return.

He stepped back realizing he had too much anger in him to do this now.

Fielding stood there for a moment facing the wall with Laurel still locked in front of him. I'm sorry." Fielding said. "Laurel, I..." Laurel moved away from him quickly to the other side of the room. "Laurel, you make me crazy sometimes."

"You have got to learn to control your emotions, Fielding."

"I thought you were going to."

" I would have never hurt you Laurel."

Fielding got up from the bed and then pulled out a cigarette went over to the French double doors to the terrace and stepped outside to smoke.

Her plan was that he would never find out about her indiscretions, but had she done it for revenge.

Yes.

It wasn't for pleasure. She didn't fall in love with Benjamin Castor. He was just at the right place when she was feeling vulnerable.

She also knew that Fielding was sleeping with Gracie while she was still there at the mansion before she left all those years ago. He had betrayed her back then. Why wouldn't he betray her when she wasn't around? Now she questioned if he really loved her or if he was still in love with Gracie. A dead woman. She was dead now and, in many ways, she was happy about that. Because she knew out of all the women her husband had been with, he loved Gracie. The others were just a ride.

Laurel knew the truth; Gracie was a threat to her marriage. Now she was beginning to think even in her death Gracie was still a threat. Was she in competition with Gracie's ghost?

"Fielding?" Gracie called out to her husband from the terrace.

Fielding was still smoking his cigarette. He turned around and blew some smoke up in the sky. She came to him out on the balcony. You have never gotten like that with me before.

Fielding looked at his wife, "I never had a reason."

Laurel had never heard her husband like this, extremely possessive.

"I just don't want you with nobody else that's all."

"We weren't together," Laurel said.

Fielding walked closer to his wife. "I don't care if you were in the land of Oz and I was on Mars, Laurel. You are mine."

Laurel felt his words hit her in the gut. She began to wonder if she even liked this new husband of hers.

Fielding walked past her after he flicked the cigarette over the balcony. Fielding was spent so he lay back down on the bed on his stomach with eyes wide open, thinking about his wife, his brother, their life, and what was ahead. And then out of nowhere as he began to close his eyes, a woman came into his dreams and began to make love to him.

CHAPTER ELEVEN

QUEEN JEZEBEL

The next day when Fielding awoke Laurel was already out of the bed. He glanced at the clock it was already 11:30 am he was in an extremely deep sleep. On any other day, Fielding was up early. He went to the bathroom showered, brushed his teeth, and dressed before he went looking for his wife. He didn't have to go far she was next door with young Spencer.

When young Spencer saw his father, he looked up from his toys and screamed out and pointed with little fingers "Daddy". Laurel didn't hear Fielding come in. The toddler was playing with only a diaper on. His chubby little body surrounded by puzzles, plastic alphabet and a few activity books. Fielding plucked him out from his toys and kissed him on the cheek.

"How are you doing this morning, my big boy?"

"Big boy" the toddler repeated.

"Yeah, you are my big boy right," Fielding said.

"Right." Young Spencer belted out now going for his father's facial hair. Fielding had been growing a beard .

Laurel got off the floor and began to walk out of the room.

"Where are you going?" Fielding called behind her.

"I see you are having private time with your son." Laurel started.

"Wait," Fielding said and put the baby down in his play area. He walked over to his wife. "I'm sorry."

She looked at him then let her eyes roll to the floor. He picked her chin up so she could look him in the eye. "I'm sorry for everything I said and everything I did. I don't know what got into me. I should have never acted that way." Fielding confessed. He dare not tell her that he had found Benjamin Castor and had him nearly beaten to death. His apology wouldn't mean much then, so he would keep that to himself.

"I won't stay here if you treat me like I'm a Jezebel."

"I know. I know." Fielding said.

Tears began to run down her face.

"Shh. Stop that. Come on." Fielding consoled his wife. "I'm sorry, I will never do that again," Fielding said now holding her body close to his.

Soon she felt more comfortable. Fielding kissed her all over her face until she smiled. Then they went back to play with young Spencer together.

Over the next few months, Fielding became a new man around the mansion. Everything was about Laurel and young Spencer. Whatever Laurel wanted she got. A trip? They went. A new chef? He hired one. A new car? He bought her a brand-new Mercedes Benz. He adorned her with gifts, diamond watch, diamond earrings, designer handbags, a gold necklace with a diamond pendant. He was treating her like a queen.

Laurel was falling in love with Fielding all over again.

Fielding saw Jake mostly on the street and sometimes downstairs in the kitchen where Jake harassed the new chef.

"Can you make me some exotic breakfast.

"Yeah, like oatmeal." Fielding chimed in.

"Shut up Field, I mean like a vegetable quiche and some well-seasoned home fries."

"Why you keep messing with the cook, man."

Fielding glanced at her trying not to show shock in her unsolicited presence or attention-grabbing appearance.

"Hello." the girl said.

"Hi yourself," Fielding replied smiling.

"I'm Demi." She said pronouncing her name De-me and extended her hand across the table.

Fielding shook her hand. "Nice to meet you Demi."

"What can I do for you?" He asked motioning for the waitress to come over.

"Nothing really, I saw you come in is all, and I wanted to meet you," Demi said. She had a raspy kind of voice like she just woken up.

"Okay." Fielding smiled, and then looked down. By then, the waitress had arrived.

"What can I get you?"

"Yes, can you get me a medium decaf coffee, black, with a little sugar," Fielding said then looked at Demi. "What would you like?"

"Ah, thanks. I'll have the same except make mine with caffeine. Lots of caffeine. Sugar and cream." The waitress laughed. "Okay, I'll be right back."

Demi leaned on the table holding her chin in her hand. "What's your name?"

"Fielding."

"Fielding what?"

"Boy, you ask a lot of questions. Let's keep it on a first-name basis for now."

"Okay, suit yourself."

"You're very beautiful- and those eyes," Demi said.

"Excuse me?" Fielding said, raising an eyebrow. "Yeah man, you're a real beauty- in a manly kind of way." Demi clarified.

"So are you," Fielding said as the waitress brought out the coffees. "Without the manly part, of course."

"I'm staring." She spoke. "I bet you get that a lot."

"No, actually I don't. "

She scoffed clearly not believing him.

The waitress returned and gave Fielding a wry kind of look.

"Mind your business," Fielding said, playfully to the waitress, before she would go in the back and start gossiping. She gave him a wink.

"Okay, sometimes I do, but I don't pay attention to it. People have asked me to pose nude and do porno films." Fielding admitted.

"I would love to see that." Demi admitted, then took a sip of her coffee.

"I'm not interested."

"Eh, look this isn't about me, it's about you. Shouldn't you be in school?" Fielding said then took a sip of his hot coffee.

"I'm out of school." Demi said and took another sip " Ow", burning her lip. "I get that all the time, I know, I look super young."

Fielding shook his head and smiled at her handing her a napkin from the table. "Really how old are you?"

"I'm nineteen."

"I don't believe you," Fielding said. "And continued drinking his coffee. "You look like you're sixteen."

"I am, I'm nineteen." Demi said sternly.

"Let me see your driver's license?"

"I don't have one. I'm working on that."

"Then let me see your non-drivers I.D?"

"I don't have it on me."

"Ha." Fielding laughed. "You're a funny girl. So, what are you doing around here, I've never seen you before?

"I'm new in the area. Do you live around here?"

"I have a condo just around the corner but I am renting it out" Fielding answered. "I come back around this way often, I love the coffee here"

She took another sip of the coffee looking at him at the same time. "It's pretty good."

"Where you stay now."

"Wow, you are quite ambitious learner, aren't you?"

"I'm just wondering, why you would leave such a fancy place, where would you go."

"I moved back in with my brother, he has a big house, plenty of room."

"Sounds like a mansion."

"It is."

Demi spit out her coffee. "No foolin'."

"No."

"You must be some big deal, huh."

"No, I wouldn't say that."

"But you wouldn't say that, even if it were true."

Fielding decided to change the subject from him to her.

"Waiting on your boyfriend?" Fielding asked.

"No, I'm supposed to meet someone is all. "In fact, I have to go- they are probably looking for me." She stood up from the table. "It was nice meeting you," Demi said, walking quickly to the door.

Fielding turned around and watched her leave. The waitress returned.

"She sure left in a hurry." She said looking through the window watching the girl run across the street.

"I know. The first time that has ever happened." It may have sounded arrogant, but it was true it was the first time a woman had run away from him, but it felt good because he did like the chase. And he hadn't done that in a long time.

Outside, Demi ran around the corner and jumped into a beautiful white Infiniti.

"You made contact.?" The woman in the front seat asked.

"Yes. I know why it took so long for him to show up at his favorite spot again." She reported.

"Why?"

"He doesn't live there anymore; he is renting the condo out."

"Did he say where he is staying now,"

"Sure did."

"Where?"

"He is back where it all started, at the mansion with his brother."

"Did he bite?"

"Of course." She said. "He's a man." Then she crossed her knobby knees and sat back more relaxed. "And ain't I a woman?"

She laughed.

The woman smiled. "Good." She coveted a drink in her hand, turned her head away, and motioned to the driver that they could leave. Her fingers were adorned with diamonds, her wrist decorated with a gorgeous gold watch.

"Tell me, was he everything that I told you?"

"Yes. But it was scary." Demi admitted.

"Scary, why?"

Because I felt like he could read my mind. He has a way about him. I had to run out of there, I get why women fall for him. He is the ultimate seductive vampire.

"I know. I've heard. I can't wait to meet him." She said more to herself than to Demi.

Fielding went home to the mansion that night wondering about the strange girl he met earlier that day, Demi. Something about the encounter felt off.

But what had mother said about strangers?

Don't talk to them.

He should have known better. He had a feeling that he would be seeing her again.

CHAPTER THIRTEEN

SOMEBODY IS WATCHING ME

"I met a girl today," Fielding told Jake.

"So what? You meet girls all the time." Jake stated slurring his words from all the alcohol he had consumed.

"No, this is different. I think she was watching me." Fielding confessed.

"Watching you what?" Jake laughed.

"I don't know. Just watching me. Following me. Waiting for me."

"You know what they say about people who think they are being followed." Jake joked. "They are paranoid."

"So, you think I'm paranoid?" Fielding asked.

"Okay, okay I'll bite," Jake said. "Where did you see this girl?"

"At the Olde Bar and Grilleolde, you know I used to go there all the time, where I get my coffee," Fielding said with a thought trying to remember any detail about her as possible. "Real pretty," Fielding said.

"Just your type. Jake said. "Tell me about her."

"We started talking. She had some coffee with me." Fielding said.

"What did you guys talk about?" "Nothing much," Then Fielding remembered.

It's the little things.

"I told her something."

"What"

"That I moved, that I was no longer living in the condo across the street."

"Why do you think she was watching you?"

"Because it's odd that she would just be there, and a young girl. I never see young ladies in there.

"Shit."

"What"

"I told her that I moved, that I was living in a mansion with my brother."

"I think someone sent her there," Fielding said.

"For what, reason?" Jake said.

"To find out where I am staying now."

"Just a feeling. It was like she had a certain amount of time to be with me, and then she had to go."

"Okay say someone did send her and somebody is following you, find out where you live, then what?"

"I can only think of one thing. Someone is feeling us out." Fielding said.

"Okay. for what?"

"To knock us out of the game. Send a chick in to test to waters. It is so fucking obvious man. I didn't want to think about it before but it could possibly be true."

"What?"

"There's a hit out on us."

"Wait a minute how did this turn into us, I thought you said she was following you." Jake said.

"Think about it, first Sean dies in a car accident.

"Then Gracie is murdered." Fielding followed through.

"You think this girl is somehow connected to Gracie's death?" Jake asked.

"Could be," Fielding said, still talking to Jake but still deep in his head thinking about this whole scenario.

"Think about it Fielding, why would someone want you dead?"

"Not just me."

"Okay, us. Why would someone want us dead?"

"It's obvious the money, the territory, our business. They want us out of the way. I don't think they know about Laurel, or my son. Probably don't know where your kids are either, we need to make sure." Fielding began talking to himself more than to his brother.

"You think they want the whole family?" Jake said. Not hearing a response from his brother, he asked, "a hit? Who do you think it is? Who would want us dead?"

"I don't know." Fielding said. "We aren't the best-liked dudes in town. I don't know, it could be linked to this Demi, girl."

"How are we going to find out?"

"Well, I was thinking- you know Alonzo. When I see this chick again, I'll get him to talk to her. You feel me." Fielding said.

"What if it doesn't work?" Jake said.

"Then we do it the old-fashioned way," Fielding said.

"What's that?" Jake asked.

"Beat the shit out of her," Fielding added, and when he said that there was nothing on his face that looked as if he was playing games.

Fielding needed to warn Laurel.

Still, Fielding was staying focused. Laurel and Spencer were now under his roof. He loved watching his son learn new words, loved hearing him giggle when he threw him in the air. Laurel smiled more now, and their nights had become tender, even peaceful. But peace never lasted long for a Damino.

Jake had been on a bender for weeks. He still used coke every day and showed no signs of slowing down. After Gracie's death, Jake lost the last of his restraint. Fielding saw him around with that same young woman. He seemed to like her more than the usual flings, but Jake was adamant: he wouldn't be tied down again. His kids remained with extended family. With the streets heating up, that was for the best.

On the morning of Day 23, Fielding sat on the terrace watching Spencer play with a toy truck. Laurel came out with a plate of fruit and set it down next to him.

"You think I'm spoiling him?" he asked, grinning.

"A little," Laurel said, taking a seat.

"I don't care. He's, my boy. I want him to have everything."

"He'll have your heart, that's for sure."

Fielding smiled but didn't answer. He was thinking. Not just about Spencer, but about his past. About who he'd been—and who he still might become.

That afternoon, Jake dropped by.

"Yo, little man's growing fast," Jake said, ruffling Spencer's curly hair.

"You good?" Fielding asked.

Jake shrugged. "High."

"You need to slow that down."

Jake leaned in; voice low. "I need to tell you something. We got a problem."

Fielding's face darkened. "Go ahead."

"I think you might be right."

"About what?"

"About everything the hit, the girl being somehow tied in with it."

"Okay, what do you know?"

"There's word out that someone new is coming for the territory. We don't know who yet. But they're not from Philly."

"Outside muscle?"

Jake nodded. "Maybe even international. These guys aren't amateurs."

Fielding felt the chill crawl up his spine. The streets weren't just dangerous—they were shifting. And in times of change, anyone could fall.

Later that night, after Spencer was asleep, Fielding and Laurel sat on the terrace again. This time, there was no laughter.

"I need to tell you something," he said.

Laurel sat up straighter. "What is it?"

"There's trouble. Real trouble. Jake says there's someone new trying to take over."

Laurel's eyes narrowed. "You think it's connected to Gracie?"

"I don't know. Maybe. But I can't let them take this from us. I worked too hard. I got too many people depending on me."

Laurel was silent.

"You and Spencer might have to leave."

"No. We just got back. You brought us here."

"And I'll protect you, but if this gets worse—"

"We'll face it together."

Fielding stood, rubbing the back of his neck. "You say that now."

"I mean it," Laurel said. "Whatever this is, we're in it together."

Fielding looked at her. He believed her. He had to. But deep down, he feared what was coming. He'd survived betrayal, death, addiction. He could handle danger.

What he couldn't handle was losing his family.

And now, more than ever, they were his only reason to keep fighting.

CHAPTER FOURTEEN

SMALL WORLD

Later that same night out on the street he saw Demi again, standing in the shadows. At first, he wasn't sure but when she looked up, he knew it was her and as soon as she made eye contact with him, she turned around and started walking quickly down the street.

"Check it out. Fielding spoke into his phone. I just spotted her, over here on West Bedford Street, not far from you guys, in fact inbound, she's coming to you."

"Follow her," Fielding commanded. "Black, jacket, black pants, light skin around 5'5".

Alonzo, Mark and Darryl. weren't too far, they were waiting on the corners, when she turned onto the street they were on, they began to follow.

"We see her, black jacket, black pants, 5'5"."

"Moving fast"

"Let's go. Alonzo commanded, Mark and Darryl, they met up from the other corners.

And started following her.

"She is headed to the club on 45th and Dobson.

She got to the entrance of the club, she was waved in, must be a regular.

She was walking in and out of people dancing in the club zig zagging her way to the back door. Alonzo had her in his sight and Mark and Darryl did too. They kept following while the music blasted, Rihanna was saying something about being in your possession the song seemed so appropriate now as the girl ran through the middle of the dancing people as the lights in the club flashed red. Then blue. Then yellow. She continued through the sea of people. Alonzo was right on her tail. She began moving faster. Her heart was racing as she squeezed through people dancing closer together in provocative dance moves. Finally, she got to the back door, she bolted through. Alonzo, Darryl, and Mark were right behind her. She was just a block ahead of them. They were quickly catching up to her. But she was a runner, Alonzo had to admit it. Alonzo was not in shape for running in fact none of them were. They were more of stand around with a gun in their waste type of hitmen, not running down the street tackle you kind of dudes.

The next block she made a turn and ran down an alleyway, that was her mistake, it was a dead-end a few doors were there along the wall frantically she began trying all of them but they led to nowhere, they had been locked down a long time ago. She kept trying them all until she spotted Darryl first somehow, he had taken the lead of the pack obviously the best one in shape. Then Alonzo now breathing really hard trying to catch his breath and then Mark brought up the rear. All three were now coming down the alley towards her.

"Pretty," Alonzo called out to her in the darkness. "There is nowhere to go." As Alonzo got closer to the runner, he saw how her curly hair laid so nicely falling all around her face, body was a small build but sexy. Alonzo, he got up on her, he brushed up on her close and pushed her up against the wall. Darryl and Mark were the lookouts at the entrance of the alley for Alonzo as he dealt with the girl. Alonzo pushed his body upon hers. If they were in an office situation no doubt Alonzo would be in violation of every sexual harassment code.

"Get off of me." She said pushing him away.

"Yeah, what you running for?" Alonzo questioned.

"What you chasing me for?" She spit back.

"Alright, let's stop playing games." Alonzo turned around and yelled to Darryl and Mark, "Call Fielding tell him our location."

He turned back and around and questioned the girl, "What are you doing around here we have never seen you before. What are you looking for?"

"I'm not looking for anything." She kept pushing him off of her.

"Who you working for pretty girl."

"I ain't working for nobody."

"Stop lying, it will be easier if you just say it. You don't want us to mess up that pretty face, do you?" Alonzo asked and then brushed up against her harder with his pelvic area. He put his tongue on her neck and licked her."

"Stop." The girl commanded.

"Stop." He said in a higher-pitched voice mocking her.

Darryl and Mark started laughing. By that time, Fielding's car was on its way down the alleyway. Fielding got out of the car and began walking towards Alonzo who still had the girl pinned to the wall.

"That's enough," Fielding commanded as he watched what was going on. When he got closer to Demi, Alonzo moved out the way. "How you doing?'" Fielding said to her. "Let's go for a ride."

Fielding had Mark drive the car and sent Alonzo and Darryl on their way back to the club.

Fielding got in the back seat with Demi.

"So, what's up who sent you to follow me?" Fielding asked.

"I'm not following you." The girl insisted.

"Stop lying," Fielding paused, "You like Alonzo," Fielding threatened, " because he likes you. I can bring him back here. You want to spend some time with him. I can call him right now." Fielding picked up his phone.

"No, don't do that." The girl said feeling cornered.

"Oh, okay," Fielding put his phone down. "You starting to remember now?"

"If I tell you this I will be in a lot of trouble."

"Yeah, I bet you will. I tell you what, you tell me who sent you to follow me and I won't tell a soul it will stay between you and I."

"This guy came up to me and asked me if you were selling, and I said I didn't know, but he wanted me to stay close to you to see if you were."

"You know what, I don't have time to fuck with you girl," Fielding picked up his phone. "Alonzo," he said into the receiver, got some fresh meat for you. That pretty little thing has decided that she wants to spend some time with you."

"Okay." She said "Grabbing Fielding's arm."

Fielding looked down at his arm. She let go. He looked into her pretty little eyes. Reading her mind he said, "I don't have any sisters. I don't give a fuck, girl."

"You got a mother, don't you?" She said.

The truth is that he did care. He didn't want that girl to get worked over by Alonzo, but he knew he had to do what he had to do to keep his business running and protect his people. If someone was following him, he needed to know exactly who it was and why. So, when this scared little girl started talking, he heard some shit that he never expected to hear.

"Confianzo me, tu es falta ir alli . Sustantivo hablar." Fielding lit up a cigarette prepared to listen.

The girl looked at him with surprise.

"Ci, Yo habla espanol. Sustantivo hablar.

Fielding had spent many nights in Miami when he was a child playing with Spanish children and his mother, the one who he thought was his mother anyway, was herself part Spanish, and Spanish became a second language for him. He didn't speak it often only when he needed to. So, they started their conversation in Spanish and as they spoke to each other she became much more comfortable with Fielding and told him what he wanted to know.

She had a lot of heart not just beauty and that was what most people felt when they saw her, it wasn't just her physical beauty it was the spirit that exuberated from her. It was strong and drew men in as quickly.

Demi was a descendant of the Seminole Indian tribes from Florida. They were the same ones who fought against the English settlers of this land and forced the natives out of Florida because of their relentless fight for the beautiful land. At the time Taft was president and he tried to run the natives out of Florida but they had joined forces with many runaway slaves hence the name Seminole as it means runaway. They fought to the death and refused to give in. The American Settlers gave them Oklahoma for Florida but there was never any real peace treaty signed. The Seminoles had fought to the death and killed thousands of soldiers and they were not retreating. That is the stock that Demi came from. She was tall with pride and would fight to the death for what she believed.

As Fielding spoke to the young girl, and learned her history he began to realize that there was something else going on here, something that Demi herself might not even be aware of, and how she had come to find herself, in Philadelphia.

The answers were startling. The more they spoke the more he realized.

It wasn't Demi who Fielding needed to be watching.

CHAPTER FIFTEEN

UNANNOUNCED

The receptionist came out to greet the woman who was waiting in the lobby for Fielding. "The woman opened the door to one of the nicest offices she had ever been in. First off, the office had a million-dollar view. She could sit for hours and just look out over the city. However, the main attraction was the ever so handsome Mr. Fielding Michaels. He was even better looking than the young girl had said. Now she understood why Demi had been so intimidated by him.

"Ms. Coleman," he said from behind a mahogany-colored desk, that shined as if it had just been polished. He stood up to greet her, "Sorry to keep you waiting."

She had been waiting in the lobby for about twelve minutes before the receptionist came out to get her.

"Alex," she replied, signaling it was fine for him to use her first name. "It's wonderful to finally meet you, Mr. Michaels."

She extended her hand. Fielding shook it gently. She noticed his Rolex, gold wedding band, and hands—strong, smooth, and impossibly sexy. His scent hit her next, and she had to check herself. She didn't like being out of control.

"Have a seat, Ms. Coleman, Alex" Fielding corrected himself gesturing to the chair opposite his desk.

"So, what can I do for you?" he asked, voice guarded.

"I think you know. You have something that belongs to me, and I want it back."

"You're going to have to give me more than that. You sent your girl to follow me—Demi, right? I know you aren't talking about her, giving her back, she does what she wants to do, you are not her keeper."

"She crossed her legs. I'm here for one simple reason. Mr. Michaels."

"And what is that?"

"Revenge!"

"You want revenge against me?"

"Yes, it's a shame you don't even remember."

"No, I don't."

"You killed my brother, you were driving down a street in Philadelphia, he was driving a black Mercedes Benz."

"Oh, I remember that day very well."

"I should be the one looking for revenge."

"Your brother tried to run me off the road. He tried to kill me."

"He was only doing what he was paid to do."

"This is incredible, so you're telling me that you are here for revenge, because of a botched hit. On me!"

"Yes, I am. It was your father who put him up to it."

"So, I want a Piece of Tattooz Inc. I want a part of this company."

"Well good luck with that. Sean's dead."

"Really. I have proof that your own father put a hit out on you, his son."

"Thanks for the DNA reprisal, I know who my father is, but it doesn't surprise me that my father may have done something like that, but it simply means that your work here is done, the hit was botched, you don't get paid. There is no compensation. Your brother knew what the consequences were when he took the job."

Fielding gave her his famous poker face, showing no emotion, no surprise, although inside he was steaming. His motto had always been never let them see you sweat.

"It's a proposal. I thought we could work together, therefore squash any beef between you and myself."

"Let me get this straight, you want to get compensated for a botched hit, that left your brother dead. And you think you are entitled to it, because my father employed him to do the job. So, kind of like a wrongful death kind of thing"

"Exactly."

"You know, you cannot make this shit up."

"Bitch are you crazy?"

"Whatever. You owe me, and if I cannot collect from your father because of his, um um she cleared her throat, untimely demise, then it is only right that I get it from you. You are his heir."

"Or what will happen if I don't "No, wait, let me guess, you are going to kill me."

"Yes, Mr. Michaels and I am. and I will."

"Good luck with that. You see where it landed your brother."

"I am not my brother."

"Well, good. But this conversation is over. You can see yourself out."

"That's fine Mr. Michaels, my business is not done with you. I'm sure we will see each other again soon."

And with that, she got up and saw herself to the door.

"Fielding spoke into the intercom to his receptionist Claire.

"Claire, I will not take any more unannounced visits, make sure everyone is screened and has an appointment."

CHAPTER SIXTEEN

REVENGE

Fielding left the office late that night. His visitor had his mind swirling. What kind of muscle did she have? Who was she representing. He still had limited information.

He decided to walk home so that he could clear his head. As he walked down the dark, dimly lit streets, he heard footsteps behind him and realized that he was being followed. Oh, not again, the thought. He checked his back for his pistol, and remembered that he did not bring it with him. He didn't panic. He kept the same pace and understood that he was in a precarious situation.

He turned the corner and the footsteps continued. There was hardly anyone on the streets at this time of night, he didn't see many cars riding up and down this particular street in fact there was only one car that rode past. He looked at the car as it slowed down. He now knew that it was a setup whoever was in that car was in cahoots with whoever the footsteps belonged. They were not too far behind him now. He continued to walk.

The next block he turned down was an alley and he had been here before he knew this alley very well. Fielding's shoes pounded the pavement he wore black slacks and a white button-down shirt. Once he turned the corner the footsteps sped up and they were on him quickly. The steps that he thought belonged to one person actually were the footsteps of two people. They were dressed in black from head to toe and pushed his face against the wall and scratched his face making him bleed immediately. There would be some women very upset about that.

"Don't move." The male voice commanded. He felt a gun in his side.

"Hey, where am I going?" Fielding said.

"Shut up, I didn't tell you to talk."

Fielding obeyed, thinking in his head as soon as he got a chance, he was going to beat the crap out of this guy.

The dude held him up against the wall with one arm while he reached in his pocket and began to make a phone call to report that he had apprehended Fielding. As soon as he did his grip was loosened Fielding turned around and punched the guy in his face which leveled him to the ground. Then another punch and hit the ground this time. He didn't move. Not dead, but out cold. Fielding now had the guy's gun turned quickly and shot the other guy two times in his chest. Blood spurt out of his body onto the pavement.

The car that had passed him, lowered down a window and began shooting at him. Fielding shot back with the gun. The car backed out and zoomed away.

Fielding picked up the phone quickly, looked around, and began walking out of the alleyway.

"Who is this?" Fielding asked into the phone.

There was no answer but still, the person did not hang up.

"Good, you want to stay anonymous, you can pick up your boyfriend he was very ineffective and he probably will have a really bad headache. The other guy was not so lucky. Next time send someone to get me who knows what they're doing." Then he took the phone and threw it back down into the dark alley and continued walking until he got to his condo apartments.

Luckily, the condo, was vacant again, so he used the condo as another residence.

When he got back home, he made a phone call to Alonzo. Alonzo answered right away.

"What's up boss?" Alonzo said into the phone as if he were just waking up.

"You sleep?" Fielding asked.

"Yeah, sort of."

"Yeah, well wake your ass up. They came at me today. They tried to take me out."

"You know who it is?"

"Absolutely. She came to see me today. claiming that she is out for revenge."

"Revenge",

"Yeah , I'll tell you about later."

"I need you to round up the boys' rights now, we gonna meet, there ain't no time to sleep. She's gonna make a move and we are gonna make ours first."

Fielding met with the boys from his team and they began to devise a plan. They were going to set up people on all corners for protection. They would have lookouts on each corner everybody would be placed on notice.

They all met down at the river. Jake came down a few minutes after they were all there, Alonzo, Darryl, Mark, and then Jake. Fielding was happy to see his brother appear out of nowhere at the riverbank. Here we can talk. They talked about how they needed to stay in touch with each other and watch each other's back because someone was out to kill them. Most likely Miss Coleman.

Alonzo, Mark, and Darryl kept watching while Fielding began to fill his brother in.

Somebody jumped me today.

"Where?"

"In an alley coming from the office."

"What happened?"

"They pulled a gun on me."

"Did you get a look at them?"

"Yeah. I shot one and the other I put to sleep. They were wearing masks I pulled them off but I didn't recognize them."

"I don't like how this sounds I am starting to think that you may be right."

"About what?"

"Someone is trying to take us out."

"You think."

"Anything strange happen with you?"

"I have been feeling lately that someone has been following me the same as you."

"Alright well look you need to get home you are kind of banged up. Why don't you go back to the mansion and get yourself together and I will meet you there I'll keep these guys on the lookout, it is too dangerous for us to be out here right now."

"What about you. You don't need to be out here."

" I am coming right behind you. You need to check on Laurel and make sure she is okay. Where is the baby."

"He's not there we were planning a night together but your right. Let me get home to make sure she is okay."

CHAPTER SEVENTEEN

ANNIVERSARY

It was Fielding and Laurel's anniversary and they planned a quiet beautiful time at home. The night air was filled with the potential of a wonderful long-lasting life together.

He had the music system play his mother's favorite song My funny Valentine, by Etta James throughout the house speakers. You could hear Etta James serenading the lovers all through the house.

He remembered when growing up with Rita Carmen he loved to hear her sing this song. She had a beautiful voice and when she thought that he wasn't listening, she would sing as if she were in front of a crowd of people. Whenever he heard it sung by the great Etta James, it reminded him of his mother. She was in love you could hear the pain in her voice.

That song now flooded every room of the mansion, you could hear it wherever you walked the kitchen, the bedrooms, the dining room, the hallways, the deep sultry voice of Etta James. Miss Etta James sang that song and became every instrument the piano, the saxophone, the trumpet, the harmonica, even the soft rumbling of the drum. The great stairway wound around as if caught up in a tornado.

When Fielding entered the mansion Laurel was standing at the top of the steps, in a beautiful flowing white gown underneath she wore a sexy panty and bra set that he couldn't wait to remove. He began walking up the stairs but as he did, he heard something outside of his house that didn't sound quite right. He took another step and heard it again.

It was the front door. Fielding turned back around as the double doors to the foyer swung open with a loud boom. Then heard a pop pop sound the only thing that Fielding could think was that they had brought the war to his home.

He could see from where he was standing that the front door had two perfectly spaced huge holes in his front door. A hole like that could have only been made with a shot gun. As he saw that he began to act quickly as time began to slow down. Fielding turned back around to his wife. He saw the look of fear on her face. There were about forty steps in between him and his wife. He wouldn't be able to get to her in time, "Laurel, run. get your gun."

Laurel turned to run for the bedroom where she kept her gun next to her bed on the nightstand. She began to hear more commotion so she closed the door to the bedroom and hid behind the bed near the window.

Fielding changed directions from going up the steps when he saw that Laurel ran into the bedroom and descended down the stairs. Right behind the great staircase, there was a huge pot with flowers in it and two pistols that he kept in case of a time such as this. He placed one in the back of his pants and the other was in his hand.

Just then the rest of the door of his mansion blew off as if a force of nature had come tumbling down on their house.

Then he saw several men begin to invade his home. One, two, three, four, five he counted quickly as they ran inside. They had on all black, faces covered with black cut out masks, and guns. They were sent by the same people who had been trying to kill him all this time and they had crossed the line because now they were in his home.

He began shooting with his pistol they returned fire back on him. Fielding could still hear the music playing in the background all around his home the voice of Etta James, his mother's singing voice calling out to him. He emptied the bullets in the one gun, hitting one of the masked intruders in the chest, blowing his chest out. He fell to the ground dead. Four left, he pulled the other gun from behind him and began shooting with it as he ran up the great stairway ducking the whole time while the men tried their best to hit their moving target.

Laurel came out from the bedroom remembering how her husband had shown her how to shoot that day and then how they came home and made love like never before. She stood at the top of the stairs and aimed then she heard her husband's voice say, *now squeeze and shoot that motherfucker.* She began squeezing the trigger and she got one of them dead on in the head. Three left.

Fielding got up the stairway Etta James was still singing, now she hit the note that he loved so much she cried into the microphone, *please stay, little valentine, stay, each day is valentine's day.*

"Laurel, come with me, it's three of them left," Fielding commanded. Laurel turned and began to run behind her husband. They ran down the hallway. A hallway that Fielding had run down before trying to save Gracie from the beating of her husband. The bullets did not stop flying, they ran down the hall until Fielding ducked into one of the bedrooms. She followed. He closed the door. When they got in the room poor Etta James's voice had been silenced. You could hear a pin drop. Laurel was scared to breathe fearing that they would hear them.

Get behind the bed, Fielding instructed his wife. Fielding went to the closet and pulled out from behind a drawer full of clothes an arsenal of weapons. He pulled out a huge gun that Laurel had only seen on television. Fielding began loading up with guns, he put another one behind his back, and now he had one pistol in each hand. Three guns. For three motherfuckers.

He heard the footsteps ascend the staircase. He went over to the door and looked out. Laurel was waiting near the bed. Stay here, watch your back, anyone come in here you shoot them, you understand.

Laurel shook her head. Still feeling like none of this was real. Fielding stepped out of the room and went down the hallway. He saw them before they saw him, and with two bullets he cut another masked man down. Dead in his tracks. Two more were coming up the steps.

He yelled at them as they hit the top of the stairs. "no one invited you, bastards, get the fuck out of my house." He said as he fired shots at them, they both scrambled.

He didn't see any more of the masked men, he ran back down the hallway and stopped at one of the men he shot, he was squirming around on the ground. He pulled off his mask. He looked familiar it was the police officer from his condo, he was there when he had the incident with Gracie. Officer Davis.

"Who sent you, who are you working for?"

"You know. "Officer Davis said grabbing his leg in pain. He grabbed his gun up from the ground.

"No, I don't' know, who, who sent you?"

Finally, Officer Davis said, the words that would change the way he felt about everything in his life. "Your brother."

Had he heard Officer Davis, right? My brother. Jake. Suddenly Fielding felt his whole insides begin to turn as it soaked in what the man had said. "Jake."

"Stay here, Officer Davis, do not move or I swear my aim will be a straight head shot."

He ran back down to the room where he had left Laurel. He got there and stopped short before entering the room. When he opened the door, he saw Laurel standing with a gun pointed at her head and none other than Jake at the other end of the gun, holding tight to Laurel using her as a shield in front of him.

"You played me this whole time?"

"Yup. Jake began to laugh this crazy vindictive laugh. That surprised Fielding "The whole time."

"All these years."

"My life was fine until you came and fucked it all up."

"You know that wasn't me, that was her, your mother, our mother, she had my mind mixed up. "

"Yeah, well just imagine how fucked up I must be I am her real child, remember, I am the bad seed."

"Jake, you are not a bad seed."

Jake looked up in the air and thought about it then said, "No, I am."

"And all that time man, you been waiting to do this?"

"You wouldn't stop, you just wouldn't stop, kept fucking Gracie, my wife, no matter what."

"Okay, she is not here anymore can we let her rest in peace?"

"I wish I could Fielding, but she haunts me every night." Jake confessed.

"Who?"

"Gracie."

"She comes for me."

"For what, what are you talking about?"

"Because she knows, but I didn't mean it."

"Mean what, Jake?"

"I didn't mean for her to die. I just wanted them to scare her, not kill her."

"Are you out your fuckin mind. You did what? You killed Gracie," Fielding said not believing what he was hearing.

"Those kids said the man who hired them, wanted her dead. That was you?"

"Everyone knew she was fucking me over. You know that. On Player's Street. You thought I didn't know about your special place, did you, Fielding. People talk. I was the joke of the day, for years. I just wanted to teach her a lesson." Jake began to break down with emotion. "I didn't want her dead. I swear I didn't, I changed my mind."

"Yeah, when you got tired of her. Man, you were cheating on Gracie, don't put that all on her. Between your beatings man, the only thing left was for her to get high. And you started her on that shit."

They could go on for hours blaming each other for the failures in their lives so Fielding realized he did play a part in Gracie's death. He could have been there for her. He put his gun up in the air. "Look man, I am putting this gun down on the ground, just let her go, laurel ain't got shit to do with this."

"Why should I let her go. Why should you get to have someone to love?."

"Let's talk about this Jake, Laurel is innocent."

"Don't matter man. She was my wife."

"I know. I tried to make up for that."

"You can't make up for shit. Can you make up for the fact that my mother, the mother you thought was yours was crazy? No, you can't. Can you make up for the fact that you slept with my wife man? No. You can't change that. Even officer Davis," Jake laughed, how do you think I got him to agree to do this shit man. You were fucking his wife too." Fielding stood there just a few feet away from his brother with fear for his wife. He thought to himself what would his son do without his mother?

"Fielding behind you," Laurel screamed out.

Officer Davis came up behind Fielding limping and pointing a gun at his back. Why did he trust that this mother fucker would stay put? Fielding turned around but it was too late, the bullet had already left Officer Davis's gun and he was hit. Fielding fell down in pain on the floor.

"Let's go," Jake said to Laurel."

One more masked guy came in the room. "Yawl okay."

Wait he knew that voice. "Alonzo?" Fielding said from the floor.

"Yes, sorry boss, it's me."

"You fucking back stabbing bastard."

"You need to know this, Fielding; we are going to kill your wife. You don't get to win this time Fielding. "Do you even know what it feels like to know that your woman is fucking another man?"

Jake stopped and looked over at his ailing brother on the floor "Oh but you do know now, don't you?"

Fielding tried to get up. He had that same fury in his eyes the night he found out that Laurel had an affair in Florida. Then he looked at his brother, with a huge question mark on his face.

"Take her" Jake commanded. Officer Davis grabbed Laurel and told her to sit on the floor in the corner and not to move.

"Yes." Jake stooped down close to the floor and began talking to his brother. Fielding was in pain where he had been shot and blood was spilling from his body. "I have to admit that little incident in Florida with wifey and the poor guy you tortured."

"You son of a"

"Be careful..." Jake warned. "Now you know that bitch was your mother too." Jake started laughing.

Fielding tried to get up to lunge at his brother.

Jake pointed his gun at Laurel who was sitting close by up against a wall with Officer Davis keeping guard. "Don't get up, you stay right there. Or I swear to God, I will kill her. Oh, what you don't like the work that I have been doing. What you think while you are out fucking everybody's wife that we would just let you get away with that?"

Jake took his foot and kicked his brother in the stomach as hard as he could. Fielding doubled back over and coughed up some blood. "Fuck you."

Jake turned around now looking at his brother with total disgust. He had Laurel by the hair, he put his face near hers and was just inches away from touching her lips.

"So, you are getting a kick out of this. Did you set it all up? The guy in Florida?"

"The guy in Florida?" Jake answered looking crazier and crazier to Fielding. "I did do that, yes, set it all up.

"I have no idea what you're talking about. I just heard about the incident from Alonzo, her overheard Jamal talking to you on the phone."

"I wish I could take the credit for that one. Priceless. But no that wasn't me. Now pulling Officer Davis in, yeah that was me, but it didn't take much because once he found out that you were fucking around with his wife, he wanted you dead. Don't you see Fielding you got so many enemies it could have been anyone that wanted you dead?"

"Yeah, well if you had done the job correctly you wouldn't have had to mess the mansion up like this. And send the girl at the restaurant and then Miss Coleman to my office."

"Oh no wait, I had nothing to do with that either."

"You don't know Alex Coleman?"

"No bro. Once again I wish I could take credit for all the bull-shit that is going on in your life right now, but I can't."

While Fielding was talking to his brother, he was busy trying to figure out how he was going to get the gun that he had in the back of his pants out before Jake decided to shoot Laurel.

Finally, Jake turned his eye from his brother for a second and began to kiss his sister-in-law in the mouth. Laurel began to resist but he held her face with his free hand leaving himself wide open for Fielding to pull out his gun and get one round off hitting Jake in the upper part of his body. Fielding got two more rounds off as Officer Davis fired back. Fielding hit him in the chest twice, this time he went down and did not move. Alonzo began shooting his pistol at them both, when Laurel grabbed a gun from the floor and began shooting one shot after another finally hitting Alonzo once in the shoulder, the leg and one last shot between his eyes.

Jake's gun fell to the ground he looked up at his brother and put his hands up in the air and smiled.

"Get over here Laurel" Fielding commanded. Laurel ran towards her husband.

Fielding walked closer to his brother. He was still standing with blood dripping from his side and his breathing becoming more and more shallow.

"Are you okay? Laurel asked concerned about the bullet wound her husband sustained.

"I'm fine. It went in and out."

I am going to check around and make sure no one is moving. You check Jake."

Laurel started checking Jake and put two forefingers on his neck to check his pulse. "He's alive." Laurel exclaimed.

Call 911. Fielding instructed.

CHAPTER EIGHTEEN

THE WALKING DEAD

It was cold now. The grounds were beautiful with the tree branches covered in white snow all the way down to the drive to the house it was picturesque. Fielding wore his boots for the snowy weather and a large warm grey coat with a furry hood. As soon as he got into the house, he began taking his coat off and plopped down on the sofa and enjoyed the heat of the home. He rubbed the palm of his hands together to draw heat faster. He blew into hands to create more heat. As he blew, he saw a pair of black shoes appear before him. He could never forget shoes like those. They were shiny, not speck of dirt on them. The man who stood in them was one of a strange cavalier type of personality. Those shoes belonged to the man that he had once dreamed of meeting and now held nothing but contempt.

He looked up from his hands and stopped blowing on them immediately.

"How are you?" A familiar voice creaked from behind a puff of smoke.

Fielding looked up from his hands slowly. Impossible he thought. But it was true, the person who was attached to those shoes, he had been to his funeral, he had seen him buried. But here he was in the flesh. His father. Sean Damino.

"When did you start smoking those?" Fielding said laying eyes on the dead man.

"Yeah, I know a different look for me, since I'm dead and all I figure I'd change the way I do things." He said in a more raspy, bizarre kind of voice not the smooth debonair quality he had remembered.

"Well, well, well." Fielding said, standing up to meet his father face to face. He wanted to make sure that it was him and not some kind of prank. It wasn't a trick. The self-made billionaire himself, stood in front of his son after all this time. It had been a while since they laid Sean into the ground. Did he know about Jake? Or Gracie. Where had he been? Who had been keeping this secret with him?

"It's good to see you too, son." Sean held his arms out indicating an invitation to embrace.

"It's good to see you too, Pop." Fielding lied, sarcastically, declining the hug. "How you been?" More than anything right now he wanted to light up a cigarette.

"I've been fine." But I should tell you that I figure I should get a new name, you know being dead and all.

"Oh, yeah. He said lighting up a cigarette. I guess we can start calling you Lazarus."

I was thinking of something more like, "Lately. Sean Lately. What do you think?" He said sitting down.

"I don't like it. Coming back from the dead. I think Lazarus fits you better you know when he came back, he was stinking to high hell.

"Touché' son."

"Lazarus it is!"

"How's Tattooz coming along."

"Great, without you."

"I'm bored. Too much sitting around. I need to get back in the game."

"The game?" Fielding said not understanding what he meant. Did he want to just walk back into the company and take over? How would he do that just walk in the office and say "Hi everyone I'm back."

"So, you finally did it." Sean announced loudly as if Fielding had just got married, or had a baby or graduated with a doctorate.

"Did what?" Fielding questioned because at this point it was all about finding out what Sean knew. He could be talking about anything.

"Tell me son, did you give your brother a good funeral, was it as touching as mine?"

Fielding gave his father a sharp look.

"He was a good boy, Fielding. Did you have to go and kill him?"

"We all know what a good boy Jake was Sean" Fielding said. "Let's see he beat his wife, drove her to become a drug addict, pissed a promising football career into the wind and yeah and let's not forget the fact that he tried to kill me and my wife."

"Uh, Uh, Uh, son…" Sean twisted his finger back in forth in the air in front of him while still holding the cigar in the other. "You were fucking his wife. She got pregnant and the paternity of Diamond is still unknown. I know she wanted to keep it that way for the sake of the family. I guess it just doesn't make sense to find out now. Still, he had to live with not knowing if that little girl was really his daughter.

"I think your brother had a good reason to want you dead, son. I was just hoping that you two would have been able to let bygones be bygones. See that is what is wrong with you, young people today you hold on to grudges too long." Sean laughed and went over to the bar to prepare himself a drink.

"I hear that Gracie is dead too?"

Fielding allowed Sean to go on and get shit off his chest before he updated his father. "I don't know where you are getting your information from but Jake's not dead, just hidden. After everything that went down at the mansion, I thought it would be best to have him lay low for a while.

"Now Gracie, she is dead. If Jake wasn't so hell bent on getting revenge, she may still be alive. I loved Gracie you know that. We both did. You just said so yourself."

"No what I said was you fucked your brother's wife. I didn't say anything about love."

She was into some hard stuff with some real bad people. I didn't even know she was in that deep. It was impossible to bring her out."

Fielding walked over to the bar and joined him in pouring himself a vodka and cranberry.

"So, was this what it was all about Fielding? You my son, come back to avenge your family rite, your family name." Fielding could now see that this was not Sean's first drink he was already toasted. Sean held his glass and cigar in one hand and flung it around in the air as he made point after point.

"This was your master plan. Get everyone out of the way and then you zoom in and become the CEO of Tattooz Inc a billion-dollar company and boom you da man. Right?" Sean said.

"No, it wasn't like that. Not after I met you, and Jake. I loved Jake. Loved you too. But Jake was into drugs hard too, he couldn't see his way out. All he knew was that I was the enemy. But when he came after Laurel, I had to make a decision. And as much as I loved my brother, Sean…. I…."

"I know…" Sean said. "Just let it go… it's over now, be thankful that you didn't kill him. You wouldn't be able to live with that." Sean's mood changed instantly from a character out of a gangster film to a wimpy old man trying to recover his dignity. It was the alcohol.

"No." Fielding said, "It will never be over. Laurel's not with me. She's gone, again."

"She'll be back." Sean stated with confidence. "They always come back." Sean laughed.

Fielding gave his father a curious look not understanding his rant.

Then within moments Sean's rant changed to silence. A quietness that could only be the procession for something even more devastating. He had been here too many times before not to have been familiar with this kind of entrance of peace so deep it could have drowned the both of them.

Finally, after the silence went on for what seemed way too long, Sean said "Do you want to know the story son?"

Sean turned back to the bar in the room and started fixing himself another drink, "You want another one?"

"No. I'm still working on this one." Sean continued to fix his drink. He poured a shot of Hennessey into a glass. The brown liquid swirled around . Damn, it now held the power that Sean was going to need to begin to tell his son a story that would surely change his life forever.

Sean took the gulp of the liquid it burned as it slid down his throat. He swallowed hard and said without turning around from the bar. "Sit down."

Fielding heard something new in his voice, it wasn't fear, or guilt, gone was the raspy speech that was there just minutes ago when they first started talking. When he accused him as being a murderous man. Now a new strange tone had emerged one he never expected to come from a man like Sean. It was a tone of sadness and shame a special kind of tonic. "You sitting down?" Sean said this time not asking but telling in a subtle, more subdued tone. It seemed that the liquor was finally doing its job.

Fielding then swallowed hard not knowing if he even wanted to hear what Sean had to say. After all the death, pain and revelations over the years he wasn't sure if he should be here.

He thought about taking the cowards way out and yell out to his father as if in some kind of drama girl/chick flick "fuck you" and then he would leave out the front door. Screaming "I don't want to hear this shit." But he didn't he stayed. He figured he hadn't gotten knocked down yet, after all they had discussed so far. Sean had thrown him out a window when he found out about his and Gracie's relationship and now, he had just confirmed his daughter-in-law was dead and his beloved Jake was tragically injured.

He was still standing he thought that right now he really had nothing to lose. He had done some real dirt in his life fucking more women than he could remember all in the name of love. In fact, he wouldn't be surprised about anything. His father had just come back from the dead, a true Lazarus, now that was epic. What the hell was he going to do for an encore.

Fielding sat down on the white sofa, reminiscent of when he first met his father and showed the picture of his mother on the fireplace radiant as any supermodel. He sat on the edge of the chair not relaxing, just waiting, anticipating the news that his father was about to spring on him.

"Sure, you don't want a drink?" Sean offered again from the bar.

Fielding smiled shook his head and then changed his mind and said, "Yeah, give me a shot of Hennessey."

Sean started fixing him a drink in shot glasses.

Sean walked over "Here you go" he said handing him the shot first.

Fielding took it to the head, sucked in his saliva then swallowed hard. It was such a smooth drink Fielding began feeling the effects of the drink almost instantly. The way he was mixing his liquors he was sure to be sick. Sean handed him the other glass. "Here run that down your throat too, you're going to need it."

Fielding accepted the second glass, thinking what was Sean talking about, the Hennessey was working Fielding was feeling pretty good right now. The fire in the fireplace was dancing . He heard some music playing in the background.

His favorite group Toni, Tone, Tony entertaining him.

Sean sat down across from his son and puffed on his cigar with the round glass of a liquor concoction that was about to take him back twenty-five years. The room began to spin and time had turned back two decades.

The sun was hidden now, the blue sky had turned black and with the help of that brown liquor with the two initials E and J, Sean went back in time. Fielding soon followed simply by his father's words he was transported back in time. Out of all of Sean Lately's short comings, he was the best storyteller that Fielding had ever heard. His love stories were the best.

"She was the most beautiful woman I had ever seen. When I first laid eyes on her my whole world stopped." He snapped his fingers. Just like that."

Fielding was mesmerized he wanted to hear the story of the woman whom he never met. The story about the woman who carried him for nine months.

Chill was that kind of beauty that you don't find every day. She had the best qualities of a woman and what I mean by that is she was down for me whatever. Ride or die.

When I saw her first, I just wanted to talk to her. I remember the day I met her. I just wanted to see her lips move. I was in love.

The first night we were together she wouldn't let me do anything she said that she wasn't that kind of woman, and that I was going to have to marry her before she could even think about getting with me. So, I got myself together and knew that I needed to go get this woman a ring. I knew right off that I wanted to marry her.

"So, I did."

Chill didn't have to try to be beautiful she just was. She was also the sweetest girl you would want to know. She was that crazy kind of lovely that never went away. You always saw it in her. I wondered what she would look like as we grew old together. I knew she would be one of those old ladies that you could tell was a looker when she was younger. I often had seen women like that when walking around town. I would see women in their sixties, still wearing high heels and legs that didn't look a day over twenty. I knew that was how my chill was going to be. Gorgeous at sixty. Hell, stunning at any age.

Sometimes she would just catch me staring at her. She could be eating cereal in the morning, or sitting in a chair catching up on one of her favorite actors in a magazine. I would just watch her eyes follow the words on the page, or her mouth chew. She would look up and ask what I was looking at as if she had no idea that I was watching her. But she would know the whole time. She just didn't want to let on that she did. I used to think those kinds of things were so charming.

With all that kindness there was a side of Chill that you did not want to unleash. It was the part of her that got hurt and then looked for revenge. I had seen that side of her once when she caught me with another girl and I didn't want to see it again. But unfortunately, I was stupid and I did it again but this time with a girl who I had wished I had never met. Rita Carmen was her name and she had a body like I had never seen. I mean ass for days and tits like two small mountains. So, when our eyes met, I knew that I was going to do the wrong thing but I couldn't help it. She was all in my mind, she was everywhere I turned. And even though I loved Chill the way I did. This was different. It was a strange kind of lust.

So, there was a bar that I went to all the time. The bar was a bit run down but we had a lot of fun in there me and Rita Carmen. In fact, it turned out that was the only place I saw Rita. She would come in pretending she wasn't looking for me. I knew she was. But I had a wife. I had a wife and I loved her. But Rita had something about her that kept drawing me towards her it didn't take long before we got together the first time it happened, we did it in one of the bathrooms of Tattooz. Then it was just about anywhere, in the alley, in the back seat of a car anywhere we were hot and heavy. I'd come home drunk and high with Carmen Rita's scent all over me.

I remember one time I came home Chill was home cooking I came in smelling something so sweet on the stove. We were living in a small one-bedroom apartment then, Sean started to laugh as he remembered. I said from the living room door, "Oh I smell something' sweet in that kitchen. I walked in there it was about nine o'clock maybe nine thirty and I saw my baby standing at the stove and came in and put my arms around her waist and she turned around and looked at me. Her eyes were a blaze. I took two steps back because I wasn't sure what was coming next. What she did shocked the shit out of me. She took that pot of food that she was slaving over and flipped it so high that all the food as if in slow motion it defied gravity and shot straight up in the air giving the ceiling a new coating of beef stew. I looked up and tried to back away before any of it hit me straight on. I had my mouth wide open that was when I realized that you don't fuck over women. The potatoes and cubes of meat began falling to the floor as if it were raining beef stew.

There was a long silence before she looked at me calmer now. "See what you made me do." She said and then walked past me and said nothing.

I remember Chill being a woman of few words her actions were so much more effective.

There was another time I came home from being out all night with Rita. She had all my shit packed up neatly on the trash. Any other woman would have thrown everything around no not my Chill. She was so deliberate with her jealousy.

So, I found out that the place was for sale. The owner Arnoldo Famoso who drank too much had drunk all the mortgage money away and lost the old bar. I was in his office one day when he was telling me his sad story.

"Yeah, Sean, I don't know how I'm going to tell my wife." Old man Arnoldo was saying.

Arnoldo used to be a good-looking man back in the day. Sitting back in his office, he had some pictures on the wall. They were all dusty now, you could tell he had put those up when he was proud to be his own business man, an entrepreneur forty years ago. Old man Arnoldo Famoso was every bit in his eighties now.

His office was dark, there was one tiny window in the corner with an old black curtain that he must have had up there since he opened the joint. This was one party place Sean thought as he listened to old man Arnoldo tell his story. I always wanted to be my own man. My daddy was a businessman he had an old moving van he picked up trash off the street when he wasn't moving people. But all he could get to work for him were a bunch of his old drunken friends so he never got the company off the ground. I said to myself that wasn't going to be me. No, I was going to be a real businessman. Look at me, Sean. Look at what happened. Then I saw Arnoldo do something that I have never seen a grown man do, Arnoldo began crying. And I don't mean that kind of cry where you holding back the tears and trying not to cry in front of someone, but those full-blown tears. Now I'm a young man sitting looking at him wondering what should I do. I just got him some tissues and hoped that he would stop soon.

So, I sat there looking at this man and saying to myself I never want that to be me. I am going to make it.

"Where is your father, Sean? Did you know him?"

"No," Sean cleared his throat." No, I didn't know who my father was. My mother said that he took off when he found out she was pregnant and she never wanted to talk about him. And guess what, I never pressed her for the information because I didn't care to know him. Sucker."

"Yeah, you say that but still it must have hurt."

"Of course, that shit hurts when your own father doesn't want to be bothered. But you know what I won't do that to my kids. My kids are always welcome in my home. I won't deny them ever."

"Remember that son."

After watching Arnoldo that day, I started to think about how could I get the dough together so I could buy that place. I could turn it into a spot that could make money." Arnoldo told me that the bank gave him ninety days to come up with the money.

I started talking to some dudes that I knew who slang dope on the street. I told them that I knew where I could sell some shit, I knew plenty of women who came in Tattooz who were always looking for dope. I told them that I could sell some shit for them if they gave me a chance. They were always looking for knuckleheads like me. Besides I heard there had just been a big bust around here most of their foot soldiers had just get sent up in the pen. I was just what they were looking for. But to do that shit, I had to get my mind right. So, I started smoking' weed, even doing' a few lines here and there. I didn't want to become an addict I just needed to get the heart to do it. So soon I was selling this dope to the females and soon as they got some and took a hit, they wanted to fuck so I did that too. I was getting deeper and deeper. Chill was getting madder and madder. I got the money though. Sixty thousand dollars, Tattooz needed work so I became the owner of the bar and I felt like the whole damn heavens had opened up for me. Right after I became an owner and new entrepreneur Chill told me she was pregnant. I was happier than a mother fucker. I was on cloud mother fucker, here I am an entrepreneur, going to be a new daddy what could go wrong.

"Never ask that question" Sean came out of his story high for a moment and looked over at his son with ghost-like eyes. "That question is a setup."

What went wrong was Rita came to the bar lounge I had changed the bar to a lounge and now it was known as Tattooz lounge, instead of a bar. She came waltzing in as if about to burst like the worst joke I ever heard she said that she was pregnant. By now I had fixed the lounge up and I had a place in the back where I would go with women I had on the side, Rita was one of those women. There were a few other rooms in the back where I made extra money on the side by having men go in the back and fuck for money. That's right prostitution I got into the oldest game in the world I was selling pussy like candy. And with Arnoldo buying houses, we were the perfect team. I was making more money on pussy than I was on alcohol. I didn't want to get into the drug game. I had done that and was lucky to get out of it besides I didn't think I had the heart . I wanted to stick with what I knew. That is what they say to stick with what you know. And I knew coochie very well.

But Rita wasn't haven't it, whereas Chill wasn't saying' much. Rita was very vocal. That day she came to tell me she was pregnant was the worst day ever.

Rita came to the back room and I was in the bar busting it up with a few friends of mine when she comes walking up in the middle of our conversation about the latest boxing match. She said she needed to talk to me. Well first of all she knew that shit was lethal. I couldn't stand it when she would act like she was my wife I had one wife and she knew how I felt about Chill. I wasn't leaving her, even though she was asking me about that shit on a regular.

I excused myself from the guys I was talking to. They started laughing' as we walked away, I think it was more because they knew what was about to go down. Rita didn't though she had no idea what she was walking into.

When we went to the back room, where there was a bed, a nightstand, and a small refrigerator that held my beer. She sat down on the bed and asked me if I loved her.

"Do you love me, Sean?" She asked as if she had no idea what this thing between me and her was.

I walked over to the refrigerator to get a beer I opened the top and took a swig. Perhaps I did that because I needed some heart I don't' know. You see back then I didn't have as much heart as I have now, and that was because I hadn't really been through anything yet.

"Get rid of it." I took another swig of beer.

"No, are you kidding? This is our baby." Rita said smiling.

I walked over to her and pulled her off the bed by her neck and jacked her up against the wall of the tiny room. "I said get rid of it." I spat in her face.

"No."

I looked at her like she was a bad omen in my life. "You will get rid of it, or I will kill you," I said to her. I mean it too. I loved Chill too much. Chill had already put up with enough from me she couldn't take this one besides Chill was pregnant too. I began clutching my hands around her throat as if she were a rag doll. "You will get rid of it"

I saw that she couldn't breathe so I let her go, she coughed to catch her breath. Once she did, she continued as if she wanted me to hurt her. "I ain't getting rid of it, you bastard."

"You will get rid of it if I tell you too, you little cunt, I am having a baby with my wife. You know the deal. You fuckin' get rid of that shit, it's not even a baby yet, what is the big deal, it's what a few weeks old." I asked her. She answered through a bloody mouth. "Yeah, it's a few weeks old."

I thought to myself, "Shit I got Chill and Rita pregnant at the same time almost exactly." I was going to burn for this.

I gave her the dough she took it then threw it back at me falling all over the floor. That was when I realized that Rita was truly in love with me. But I didn't love her. At that time, I just felt sorry for her, she knew what was at stake here, no one told her to fall in love.

I roughed her up a bit more and then kicked her out told her I didn't want to hear from her again until she got rid of the baby.

The next time I saw her, she said that she had done it, I believed her. But then shortly after that Rita disappeared. I was so busy with customers, making money, and getting ready for the baby with Chill that I forgot about Rita. I didn't even realize that she had faded into the black until Chill had the baby, the baby that was you.

You know the rest son. Sean walked around with his drink in his hand as if he were a king. But there are some things that you don't know, my boy. Sean began to chuckle. It wasn't just any kind of chuckle it was sadistic. You are not the only one with secrets. Sean shook his finger at his son.

"I am what I am Fielding. And you are right I'm fucked up but I got a reason for that, don't you think?"

"You want to feel sorry for yourself go right ahead. I ain't got time to live in the past." Fielding continued towards the door.

"Chill didn't just have a car accident." When Fielding heard those words, he stopped dead in his tracks.

"What do you mean?"

"She killed herself Fielding. Kind of ironic isn't it with what Jake's mother did and all."

"You know what you use people Sean and I don't believe a word that you are saying. You are a fucking nut you need to be getting some treatment because you are crazy. You have been carrying this around with you for years and now you expect me to understand this shit.

***

So, when she walked out from another adjacent to the living room. Fielding stepped back when he saw her. She was tall, slender.

Sean laughed when he saw his son's face.

"Alex, what are you doing here? Fielding said very slowly, calmly trying to process what was going on.

"Ah, you know this woman?" Sean said smiling.

"We've met."

"You may want another drink son," Sean said.

"Yeah. well," Sean said. "I told you that today was the day for confessions."

"Well, then no need for formal introductions then. You know the man that you tortured to death." That was Alex's brother.

But what you don't know is that Alex is your half-sister.

"Why didn't you stay dead?"

"Yes." Sean slapped his legs and stood up. "Brilliant isn't it. A long-lost sister, I didn't even come looking for her, she found me." Fielding looked from Alex to Sean. "Oh, you look confused son. She was looking for you but found me instead and when I heard what you had done to her poor brother."

"You think you are so smart; she is playing you Sean. This woman is no more my half-sister, than she is your daughter. You, win Daddy, you get the award for creating the most fucked up family." Fielding said.

"This woman is a fraud, Sean. God how he wanted a cigarette right now. But he would use restraint. He also wanted to pull out the pistol that he kept in the back of his pants but he didn't do that either.

No, the punishment that his father had come to him would be even more severe than a bullet to the brain. It would be something so subtle that he wouldn't even see it coming.

Fielding picked up his phone and made a phone call. "Demi can you come over to the mansion, right quick."

"Who is that?"

"Yes, you would like to know. Wouldn't you? You know it is pitiful that you don't even know your own children. People can just walk up to you and tell you anything.

"That's what you did, you just showed up on my doorstep."

"Yes, but I had proof. What did she have? Sean, Nothing. She was behind a hit on your son, she got her brother killed and then came up with some lame story that she was your long-lost daughter when she found out that you really did have a daughter, named Demi. Rita Carmen's second child that you had with her, after you got her pregnant the first time, you went back and did it again. Tell the story correctly Sean, if you are going to tell it. You didn't even know Rita Carmen, she had told me so many stories about her history, where her family was from and how she was a descendant of the Seminoles. How she came to speak Spanish, how I had learned Spanish, you didn't even know, you knew nothing, you didn't even know she had another child. She hid two children from you, Dad. Not just one"

"You screwed over my mother, and she was fed up with you and your lies and that is why she got away from your lying ass."

Demi popped up in the living room, as they were talking. Alex sunk down into the sofa, not knowing which way to go.

"Hi Dad" Demi said, and waved. Standing next to her brother, Fielding.

"See unlike you Sean, I do research. I check out what people say, I just don't believe everything, if you can't trust family, who can you trust. Sean.?"

"But, tell me, why play dead?"

"The company was losing money and contracts, I needed to disappear, and I needed the money, if I was alive, it was no way I could have collected my life insurance money."

"And that is where Alex Coleman, comes in, she helped you get that money."

"I couldn't very well have walked into the bank and got it on my own."

"So, you knew, she wasn't your daughter. You knew the whole time. You guys were in this scam together. I didn't think you could do it, but this is a whole new low for you.

No need to worry about the company Tattooz is doing great."

"I wanted to save the company. I thought me dropping out of the picture and having my son in charge would make for great news in the papers."

Sean looked at his son. You think I am going to let you take the legacy of Gracie and my son, from them.

"You said it yourself. I didn't kill Gracie, Jake did."

"But it was because of you, Fielding. You provoked him."

"I was his excuse for being a bad husband. He brought this on to himself. Before I ever came into the picture, he was beating on Gracie and you know it."

"You think I am going to just let you do this to me. You come here with vengeance in your heart and then I'm supposed to what. Respect you?"

"No, you were supposed to love me. But you never did and you can't because you are just that kind of guy, Dad. "Fielding said and walked closer to his father. The closer he walked he didn't care what Sean would do to him. He didn't care if he pulled out a gun."

Sean continued , scoffed at Demi, "You think this little girl is ready to run a company? With you leading her around by the nose I'm sure it will sink."

"Alex, he came looking for you right?" She shook her head yes. He will use you just like he used me, Jake, and our mother's and everyone else that came into his life. You know, you are dead too, you just don't know it yet.

Alex scoffed and shot a look at Sean.

Fielding turned to Sean, "I know I wanted to know everything about your existence and now I guess I do. You were right about one thing Fielding said placing the glass back on the counter of the bar. I definitely needed that drink."

He took one last look at the mansion where he knocked on the door for the first time as a young teenager, he had come there to settle a score a fight that was not his, and yet he had been born into the middle of it. Now he needed to step up and get his family back. Sean had tried to strip him of everything. But still, he had been careless with his love. He had been careless with his son. He had let the thirst for money and power take over and that was the last thing that he wanted to be was his father's son.

And with that Fielding walked out of the door, with a new sister. And the hope that he would never lay eyes again on the man that he once knew as father but now would only remember as Lazarus.

CHAPTER NINETEEN

NEW TENANT

The morning was brisk, fall was in the air. He walked down the steps to his condo down to the light and crossed the street. He walked to the Olde Bar and Grille He became very calm as the aroma of coffee embraced him.

He purchased a medium cup of coffee, decaf. He sat down at a table by the window. As he peered out the window he watched as a woman met up with a man on the street opposite the coffee shop. They gave each other a kiss before they walked into the restaurant on the corner. He thought about how he wished that was he and Laurel. Just a few doors down the street there was a homeless man with a sign that read Veteran need food. People just walked by him as if he was invisible. A bus rolled down the street full of people going shopping or stressed to get to work on time. A woman walked by with her little son talking to him he could tell by the look on her face that she was chastising him. Two men walked past the window of the coffee shop holding hands and laughing out loud together enjoying a private joke. Then a white man with a suit and his briefcase walked by in a hurry perhaps late for a meeting. Fielding sipped his coffee feeling like this was a brand-new day.

As he turned back around to face the table, a young girl slipped in the chair in front of him. It was Demi with a huge smile on her face.

"Hi there, big brother."

"Hi yourself."

"I thought you wouldn't make it."

"Nah, I wouldn't miss this meeting for the world."

"Well, what you got them bags for, you moving?"

"I think so, I can't stay with that identity stealer."

"I get it."

"Just so happens, I have a condo available across the street."

"Really, just across the street." She giggled.

"He pushed the key over the table to her."

"Really." Demi smiled. "Are you for real."

"Yeah, I'm for real. Just don't make a mess.

"Go on get settled inI've got some things to take care of."

As he stood in the doorway of the old bar and grille a woman walked by smoking a cigarette, he got a whiff of the sec-ond-hand smoke it smelled good to him as it filled his lungs with that good ole' poison. God how he wanted a cigarette but he wouldn't get one. He wouldn't succumb to the pressure of his greatest bad habit he would continue to walk past every store selling cigarettes and every person smoking on the street he would restrain himself. He knew he could do it as he stepped out onto the sidewalk with everyone else in the world.

CHAPTER TWENTY

MY FLOWERS

First stop of the day was visiting the hospital where Jake was still recovering from his wounds.

The machines and tubes were gone now, he was a lot stronger, it had already been months, and it would be months more that Jake would need to recover and he thought this would be the best place for that to happen.

"Hey Bro." Jake said.

Fielding didn't respond. He walked over to the side of the bed. "You know you are lucky to be alive, you fuckin fuck."

"Oh, wow, your cussing is getting really bad, Fielding. Sloppy."

"You turned my men against me, for what? Gracie's dead because of you. Because of your mishandling of her. You got her hooked-on drugs. You got her killed."

"They weren't supposed to kill her. Just scare her a little."

"Yeah, well that's what happens when you send amateurs to do dumb shit."

"How's Laurel?"

"Don't you even say her name." Fielding said. "She's gone again. I can't keep her safe. She is not safe around us. You know why?"

"Because we are a couple of swell dudes."

"Because this whole family is crazy. Sean faked his own death. Did you know this mother fucker was alive?"

"I suspected he was. I heard rumors."

"Yeah, well thanks for letting me know. I nearly shit myself, when I turned around and he was standing there, I thought I was seeing a ghost."

"There is something else."

"What?" Jake tried to sit up.

"There is another sibling,"

"What?"

"Yeah, we have a little sister."

"You know the girl who I told you about?"

"Yeah."

"I did some digging. I found out that Sean had another child, in Florida.

"The   girl   you   said   was   following   you."
"Yes, even though she was put up to it, but they knew and tried to use her to flesh me out, and eventually use her to get their hands on Tattooz. All orchestrated by Sean Damino.

"Yeah, she's going to stick around, I'm letting her stay in the condo."

"Okay, family. How is therapy did you make your 23 days clean?"

"I did, finally, and then Sean goated me with some drinks, and I did drink some, but I didn't want any more after that. I even went on a long walk back to the Old Bar and Grille and didn't smoke a cigarette.

"Oh, man, that is fantastic. I knew you could do it."

"And so can you."

"I don't know Sean, if I have it in me."

"You do, trust me, we have the same DNA, you can do it."

"What about the women?" Jake asked.

"I'm still working on that one." Fielding said.

"How are you going to stop him?" Jake asked.

"Who?" Fielding said.

"Lazarus."

"I already have that figured out."

"You care to let me in on it."

"Not right now, but soon enough."

"I'm surprised that you trust me again."

"Yeah. I do. This is the thing though, if you go against me again, brother. I swear to God. Next time, I will kill you."

Jake laid back in the bed. He had no response to that promise. He let his brother's words sink in.

Fielding's phone rang, hey man I got to go. it was Laurel.

"Let me call you back as soon as I get in the car."

"I will see you tomorrow." Fielding told Jake.

Fielding got in the car and connected his phone to the speakers and called his wife back.

"How are you?"

"I'm fine, just got finished checking on Jake."

"How is he?"

"He is okay. He'll make a full recovery. I got a surprise for him.

"What's that?"

"I got him a private nurse."

"A private nurse."

"Yeah, I remember when I had a private nurse, how that blossomed into something beautiful."

"Yeah, it sure did." Laurel agreed.

But you know, now seeing Sean is still alive and Jake almost dying it makes me realize."

"Realize what?"

"That I want my flower's now, Laurel, not when I'm dead. What good are then?"

CHAPTER TWENTY-ONE

ANNOUNCED VISITS

Friday morning, Fielding came into the office early. There was a woman there waiting for him.

His receptionist, called him on the intercom.

"Mr. Michaels there is a Ms. Monica Weldon here to see you, sir."

"Monica?"

"Yes, sir. She said she is from Brockton and Sire" She made an appointment, I put it on your calendar.

"Oh, from the marketing group, fine, send her in."

In a few moments his receptionist was peeking her head in the door and then giving the woman the okay to enter.

Ms. Weldon was stunning in a blue pin stripped pant suit with a light blue blouse underneath and a beautiful black side tie across her neck. Her hair had a part in the middle with a neat pony tail that draped down her back. Classic and sexy. She looked like a modern- day Sade, reminding him very much of the woman they called Chill, his mother.

"Mr. Michaels it is so good to meet you." Ms. Weldon said as she extended her hand across the desk.

"Likewise." Fielding's voice became soft, fascinated by her beauty.

"I am here to discuss your company doing business with Brockton and Sire, as the new marketing group for your brand-new gaming device."

"I'd love to read your firms proposal. You can leave it here with me."

"Okay." Ms. Weldon said, feeling disappointed that Fielding didn't want her to at least give her elevator pitch that she had prepared.

She took a folder out of her bag and placed it on his desk in front of her.

"Thank you." Fielding said to her with a poker face.

"My pleasure." Ms. Weldon tried her best to recover her emotions without Fielding being aware, but it was too late. He read her, and new exactly where he stood.

In a few days Fielding had Claire send a message to Ms. Weldon for her to meet him at a restaurant in the North Eastern part of town.

It was a beautiful restaurant that Fielding frequented, he had a private room. He was already waiting for her, when Ms. Weldon arrived. She was looking even more lovely than the first time he saw her in the office. This time wearing a flowing dress that moved with her body. Showed some leg and lots of cleavage. Feilding stood up as she approached the table and sat down after she was seated. Ms. Weldon was impressed, a gentleman.

"I read the plan and I am in. It's brilliant. This new project that *Tattooz Inc.* is presenting to the world will go well with your marketing plan. Let me show you."

Fielding got up from the table, held his hand out to Ms. Weldon to get up she accepted his hand. Then he escorted her to the window. They were very high up in the building, the restaurant overlooked the entire city. Fielding stood closely behind her as he spoke in very close to her ear.

"We can rule this city."

Ms. Weldon turned around quickly, now facing Fielding."

"Mr. Michael's I'm married."

"I know." Fielding said. "So am I". He looked at her with those beautiful brown eyes, then he gently took his hand and lifted up her chin and kissed her with his soft beautiful lips.

She was all in.